THE SLEEPING STONES

THE SLEEPING STONES

Beatrice Wallbank

Firefly

First published in 2023 by Firefly Press
25 Gabalfa Road, Llandaff North, Cardiff, CF14 2JJ

www.fireflypress.co.uk
Copyright © Beatrice Wallbank 2023

The author asserts her moral right to be identified as author in
accordance with the Copyright, Designs and Patent Act, 1988.

A CIP catalogue record of this book is available
from the British Library.

1 3 5 7 9 8 6 4 2

ISBN 9781915444059

This book has been published with the support of
the Books Council of Wales.

Typeset by Elaine Sharples
Printed and bound in Great Britain by
CPI Group (UK) Ltd, Croydon, CR0 4YY

MIX
Paper | Supporting
responsible forestry
FSC® C171272

For Bridget, Bob and Becky,
the other three Bs.

Chapter 1

Dear Griffith (is that how you spell it?)

*My name's Mat, which is short for Matylda. My mum is
Zofia Kowalska (but everyone calls her Zosia) and my
stepdad is John Taylor, and we live in Manchester but
we are about to move into the house next door to you.*

*My teacher Miss Awad said it might be a good idea to
tell you I exist. I think you probably already know I exist
because your dad met my mum and John. I think Miss
Awad is more worried about me moving than I am.*

*My mum and John make websites and my mum is
going to be joining your lifeboat crew (she used to do
it when I was small and we lived by the sea). I'm going
to be an oceanologist: someone who studies things that
live in the ocean. I can't swim but I want to learn. I love
the rain and I don't like really hot days or broccoli.*

from Mat

Gruffydd read the letter again. Matylda – Mat – hadn't spelt his name right, but he guessed she'd only heard it said. To be fair, he wouldn't have guessed her name had a 'y' in it. His stomach did little nervous hops at the idea of the New Neighbours moving in today. Gruff didn't like change, but it seemed like everything was teetering on the edge of change at the moment. Like the beginnings of a cliff-slip, he could feel small stones shifting beneath his feet, ready to send him on a headlong plunge into the sea. It wasn't the New Neighbours' fault they were moving on to the island when Gruff's family were struggling to stay. But it still felt unfair.

Gruff stuffed the letter in the pocket of his jeans and watched Dad and Hywel the collie dog round up the sheep in Bottom Field below him, the sea sparkling in the sunlight beyond. James was finishing setting up the shearing equipment in the barn and Ffion stood in the field a little way away, rattling a bucket of nuts to encourage the flock to follow her into the temporary pen they had set up. James and Ffion always came to help on shearing day, and any other times Dad and Nain needed an extra hand. Although they were much older than Gruff, they were two of his best friends. *If the farm fails*, Gruff found himself thinking, *James and Ffion won't have jobs here anymore*. Would that mean James and Ffion wouldn't have enough money to stay on the island either?

He pushed the thought away and concentrated on his current task: to guard the gap between the temporary pen and the farmyard. As Ffion turned and led the sheep towards the pen, shaking the bucket encouragingly, Gruff readied himself for the inevitable. There was always one.

Today, that one was Guinevere.

On the whole, the flock was resigned as they trooped into the pen after Ffion and her nut bucket, but Guinevere was having none of it. In a sudden surge of speed, she charged for the freedom of the farmyard.

Gruff flung himself sideways and grabbed for Guinevere's fleece, but she barged past him like a champion rugby player and sent him sprawling on the muddy, hoof-churned ground.

'Sheep out!' Dad shouted, walking at the back of the flock.

'On it!' Gruff called, leaping to his feet. He wiped his mucky hands on his even muckier jeans and raced after Guinevere's retreating woolly form.

Hens scattering before them, Gruff chased Guinevere across the hard earth of the yard and out onto the coast path. Wildness was in her hooves and she led him along the wide, sandy sweep of the beach and past the cluster of lime-washed fishermen's cottages. Three-year-old Prem was laughing and waving to them over his garden wall and old Iolo was hanging out his washing in the breezy sunshine.

Guinevere veered off to the right, up the steep scramble of the footpath to the headland at the end of the beach. With nowhere left to go but the sea, she finally stopped running. She turned to face Gruff and did a wee, staring at him like a petulant toddler.

'All right, Guiny,' Gruff gasped, clutching a blossoming stitch. 'The great escape's over. See, you're panting, you impossible sheep. You'll be much more comfortable when you're not carrying all that fluff.'

He took a step towards her, but Guinevere danced sideways and almost lunged past him again. Gruff backed up. If she got past him here she could lead him a proper dance, all round the island. Better to keep her on the short spit of headland and wait for her to calm down.

A stone's throw away from Gruff, a seal bobbed its head up from the waves, looked around, and disappeared again. A tern skimmed the swell, searching for fish, and the breeze ruffled the short, coarse scrub of the headland. With one eye on Guinevere, Gruff looked out at the glimmering water and tried, for a second, to imagine not being here.

He did this sometimes: an attempt to catch himself unawares and see if he could get used to the idea.

He couldn't get used to it. The very thought squeezed his heart so tightly he could hardly breathe.

Gruff glanced at Guinevere, busy grazing on a clump of pink thrift. She eyed him sideways, daring him to try any funny business. Gruff smiled and looked back the way they had come, down the long, low sandy beach towards the lush, green sweep of Bottom Field and the grey stone of the farmhouse and barns.

His eyes were drawn to the Sleepers. No one could look along the beach and not find their gaze resting on those six stones, dark against the shining sea. They led out from the land, heading for the far horizon as though they were the stepping stones of giants.

Gruff imagined the journey out along them. The dangerous jump between each, leaping across choppy white-flecked water; the triumphant arrival on the last stone, arms spread wide to catch the wind between his fingertips. Nothing between him and the mainland.

If his grandma, Nain, were to be believed, no one could stop at the final stone. The Sleepers would tempt you into one more leap, and the waves would close over your head and the current would sweep you away.

Stepping stones to the bottomless ocean.

Nain would be cross with him for just imagining climbing out on them.

A warm, rough nose knocked against his hand. Gruff looked down and grinned. Guinevere had forgotten she was meant to be running away and had come over to see if he had treats.

'You're in luck,' Gruff said. From his hoodie pocket he pulled the stale crusts of bread he had grabbed from the bread bin that morning, guessing (rightly) that shearing day would require some sheep-bribes. Guinevere gobbled one up and nosed for more.

'Maybe,' Gruff said, 'you'll get some more if you come back with me and take your coat off.'

He turned and began to walk back the way they had come, his hand held in a loose fist at his side – an empty fist, but tantalising to a hopeful sheep. Guinevere followed.

As they left the headland, Gruff glanced up at the Sleepers again. They held his eyes. He paused and watched the swell surge around them.

The Sleepers are hungry and the sea is waiting.

Just an old line from an old story. But there were times when the temptation pulled as though he were connected to the stones by a thread; when they seemed to hold his gaze far stronger, far longer.

Guinevere bumped against him, impatient for more bread. He glanced down at her, then back up again.

There was a figure, standing on the final stone.

Gruff's heart thumped, hard.

Tall and upright, the person stood there. Just stood. Arms at their side, staring out to sea. A long coat – a cloak? – flapped in the breeze behind them.

Scudding clouds hid the sun, and grey light swept in from the water. The stale smell of seaweed round the base of the headland and the fresh tang of salt in the leaping spray seemed suddenly stronger. It caught in the back of Gruff's throat and flicked across his tongue, tasting of hidden places under the water.

No one could have had time to jump along the Sleepers from the beach in the half-second when he'd glanced down at the sheep now nibbling his fingers.

Gruff blinked salt-dry eyes and the stones were empty. Rounding the end of the island beyond them was a small yacht. The mast and sail were a tall, thin shape against the white-blue morning sky.

He relaxed. Mystery solved. He'd seen the boat, lined up with the stone, and imagined a person. A trick of the light and the glittering sea.

But as he led Guinevere back past the beach and through the farmyard, Gruff found the sight still lingering in his mind, like the after-image from the flash of a camera. Something was wrong. He couldn't put his finger on what, but it was the same sort of feeling he got when Dad had been into Gruff's bedroom to steal back the sellotape or return a book that had been lent to Prem. Tiny differences that told him someone had been in there, even if he couldn't work out exactly what had changed.

Something was wrong about that after-image in his mind's eye. Something was not as it should be.

Chapter 2

Eighty-nine sheared, rolled and packed fleeces later, Gruff stood beside Dad on the jetty near the lifeboat slip. Together they watched Dai's small fishing boat, *Molly*, rear up and down in the swell under a grey, late-afternoon sky. Gruff's stomach danced with nerves.

Mat was going to be the only other eleven year old on the island, and Gruff knew everyone expected him to make friends with her. But he didn't know how to be friends with someone his own age. He was used to his friends being adults, like James and Ffion, or very small children, like three-year-old Prem or two-year-old Steph. Now he was going to meet the girl who had written that confident letter, who wanted to be an oceanologist and didn't like broccoli. He had to think of something to say.

He hoped he didn't smell too strongly of sheep.

Dai steered the boat into the bay. Out on deck, framed by a mound of luggage, stood the New Neighbours. The man and woman – John and Zosia – were looking out towards the jetty; they waved and

Dad waved back. The girl next to them – Mat – did not look up. She was gripping the rail tightly and staring straight down at the water as it chopped and churned. Gruff wondered if she was feeling sick. Looking at the horizon helped that, not staring at the sea.

Dai cut the engines and leapt from the wheelhouse as *Molly* drifted in to bump her fenders against the wooden planks of the jetty. He chucked the stern mooring rope to Gruff, who looped it round the nearest bollard. Spray peppered his muddy jeans with dark drops of seawater. Further down the jetty, Dad caught the other rope and *Molly* came to a gently rolling halt. Mat was still staring down at the water, strands of light brown hair escaping from her two plaits and whipping behind her in the brisk breeze. She had not once looked up.

John and Zosia left the rail and picked up a rucksack each.

'Good crossing?' Dad called as Dai started to loosen the holding ropes round the luggage.

'Not bad,' Dai replied, and Gruff saw him give a little wink and flick his eyes towards John, who was tall, dark-haired and, currently, looking distinctly green round the gills.

Zosia, who was much shorter and had fair hair and a big, genuine smile, jumped off the boat with sure sea-legs and held her hand out to Dad. 'Nice to see you again, Owain.'

'You too,' Dad said. 'Welcome to the island – *croeso.*' He turned to the boat. 'Let me help you ashore, John. You look like you need some land under your feet!'

John clambered off the boat with much less grace than Zosia, and Gruff tried hard not to smile at the look of utter relief in the man's eyes.

'My son, Gruffydd,' Dad said, and all eyes turned to Gruff. He felt heat rising to his face and was suddenly aware of his muddied jeans and the holes in his hoodie.

'Hi, Gruffydd,' Zosia said, coming over and holding her hand out. Gruff shook it, feeling awkward. He noticed her unchipped, blue-painted fingernails and the dirt that lingered beneath his. But then he looked up, and her smile was so wide and beaming that he found himself smiling back.

'Nice to meet you,' John said, coming over and shaking his hand as well. He had a strong Scottish accent. John was taller than Dad and Gruff had to tilt his head back to look up at him properly.

'Matylda!' Zosia called. 'Come and meet Owain and Gruffydd.'

Mat jumped, turning from her sea-gazing as though she had just woken up. She glared silently at her mum and Gruff felt a combination of satisfaction and sympathy that she seemed just as uncomfortable as he had felt when Dad had drawn attention to him.

Mat shouldered a pink rucksack with a dangling minke whale keychain.

'Hi, Matylda,' Dad said, as Dai helped her step ashore. 'I'm Owain, and this is Gruff.'

Mat flicked her gaze up at Gruff and his heart kicked in his chest with surprise. Something in her brown eyes seemed to be moving with the leap and surge of a mounting wave, as though the sea was inside her and about to break out.

Gruff took a step backwards, fighting a sudden, mad urge to run away.

Mat blinked and her eyes were calm and steady, nothing unusual about them at all. *Molly* bumped softly against her fenders and red-billed oystercatchers shrieked to one another across the shoreline rocks. All was as it had been.

'Hi,' Gruff said. The sound of his own voice pulled him back to reality, and the moment before seemed far-off. 'Nice to meet you.'

'You too,' Mat said quietly. She fiddled with one of her plaits. She didn't look like the bold, confident girl Gruff had imagined from reading her letter.

The first of the big bags was heaved over the

side by Dai, landing on the jetty with a thud. The awkward introductions melted into activity as Gruff helped unload the boxes and bags off *Molly* so that Dai could head round the island to his berth at Trefynys. The adults talked and laughed as though they had known one another for years, but Gruff kept quiet, not knowing what to say and wanting Mat to seem more friendly. She was silent, but Gruff caught her glancing at him a couple of times. He felt he ought to start some sort of conversation but the words wouldn't come. *This would be easier if she was three*, he thought. *I know how to be friends with three-year-olds.*

He slid his gaze sideways at her again and again, but didn't see even a hint of what he had imagined before – that surging power, the sea in her eyes. It must have been a reflection from the waves. What with this and the person-on-the-Sleepers, his imagination was obviously having a field day.

At last the bags were unloaded off the boat and half of them were piled high in the hand-cart Dad and Gruff had brought with them. *Molly's* engine spluttered into life and she was off, round the island towards the harbour at Trefynys.

'We don't have a quad bike,' Dad explained as he took one handle of the cart and John and Zosia took the other. 'We try to be as fossil-fuel-free on the farm as we can. Solar panels and wind turbines, you know? You can get electric quad bikes now, but not in our price range! That's what Evan Williams has, though – cow farmer, and barley, most of the fields on the island are his. Lovely man. You'll meet him at the festival tomorrow. He wanted me to tell you that he was going to lend you his quad for the move, but unfortunately it's out of action at the moment.'

'No worries,' Zosia laughed. 'I like this. It's an adventure!' The three of them heaved and the cart began to trundle behind them on its thick-rimmed wheels.

'Bring some smaller stuff,' Dad called back to Gruff and Mat. 'We'll come and make a second trip for the rest.'

Looking panicked to be left alone with Gruff, Mat started sorting through boxes.

'What should I take?' Gruff asked.

Mat shrugged and shook her head. 'Shouldn't we stay?' Her voice was so quiet Gruff barely caught the words.

'Why?' he asked.

She frowned. 'Because someone might take the stuff?' Gruff could hear an accent in her words now that wasn't her mum's or John's – he guessed it was a Manchester one.

'Oh,' Gruff said. 'Nope. No one would do that. And if they did, everyone else would know about it.'

'Oh … right.' Mat looked unconvinced, but she grabbed a small cardboard box and held it out to him. 'It's only got the kettle in it. It's not heavy.'

Gruff took the box. Mat grabbed another with 'toaster' scribbled on it in biro, and they headed up the jetty towards the shore. The wooden planks gave way to the earth of the coast path. The cart trundled on ahead of them, the voices of the adults mingling with the sound of its heavy wheels.

Mat took a deep breath as though she was about to speak, but didn't. After a moment she tried again, her words tumbling out of her in a rush. 'If we don't take the kettle now, Mama and John can't have tea, and I think that'd make their world end.'

Gruff grinned. Mat smiled shyly down at the freshly-made handcart tracks in the mud.

'That sounds like Nain,' he said. Nain was a great believer in tea.

'Nine? Nine what?' Mat asked.

'Grandma,' Gruff said. 'It's Welsh for grandma.'

'Oh, right! I call my grandma Babcia.'

They fell silent again, but this time Gruff didn't mind the silence so much.

Chapter 3

Gruff and Mat came round the base of the headland where Gruff had cornered Guinevere that morning. The yellow-grey sandy beach stretched out before them.

Mat gasped and stopped stock-still. Before Gruff could ask what was the matter, he found his gaze dragged away from her to the distant Sleepers: sharp and dark and dangerous. They pulled at his chest.

'*Peidiwch*,' Gruff said out loud. Don't.

The pull vanished and he shivered, angry with himself. What was wrong with him today?

'Those stones are amazing,' Mat said, not taking her eyes off the six hulking shapes.

'They're called the Sleepers.'

'They look like giant stepping stones,' Mat breathed.

Unease crept into Gruff's heart. 'Everyone thinks that, but you mustn't try. They're dangerous.'

Mat laughed. 'Dangerous? They're just rocks.'

'They're slippery. The waves get really wild out on the end, even if it's calm by the beach. And the current is strong and it'll pull you under.'

'Only if you fall in.'

'You *will* fall in, that's the point – it doesn't matter how careful you are, Nain says. Anyone who climbs on those stones will jump out to the end, and then they'll jump in the sea. The Sleepers lure people.'

Mat smiled and continued along the path towards the fishermen's cottages and the beach, clutching the toaster box to her chest. 'That sounds like a story to keep little kids safe.'

'It's not just that,' Gruff said, annoyed. Who was Mat to dismiss his Nain's warnings as though they were unimportant? 'Islanders have told stories about the Sleepers for generations. It doesn't matter how old you are. The sea's always dangerous, and so are the Sleepers. Can't you...'

He broke off, gritting his teeth to stop the words escaping. *Can't you feel their pull?* he'd been about to say, but she'd probably just laugh at him. The island had its old, old stories, and he had seen more than one tourist laughing in Nain's face.

Besides, Gruff knew the pull of the Sleepers was just imagination strengthened by the stories about them. You were told that they lured people, so you felt their lure.

'Sorry,' Mat said suddenly.

'What?' Gruff asked, confused.

'I think I've annoyed you. I didn't mean to.' Mat's voice was very small.

Embarrassment washed over him and he shook his head. 'Oh. Sorry. No. I just...' He petered out, feeling bad. He was meant to be being friendly, and she seemed nice enough. 'Um ... you said in your letter that you lived by the sea before, right? The sea's great but it's dangerous too. Sorry if I sounded mean. I was just trying to help.'

Mat gave him a shy smile. 'We lived by the sea in South Wales until I was five,' she said. 'Mama volunteered with the lifeboat there. Then she met John – he was on holiday – and we moved to Manchester with him. I love the sea. I remember paddling. Mama says I was always trying to go out too far, even when I was really small. I guess I should be more sensible now I'm older. I'm allergic to chlorine in swimming pools so I haven't learnt to swim. I really want to learn, though.'

They were past the fishermen's cottages now, and Top Field stretched to their right, full of newly-shorn sheep. Thundering hooves approached and Mat leapt back as Guinevere careered up to the wall and stuck her nose over the top, hoping for more bread.

'Sorry, Guiny,' Gruff grinned. 'No more bread for you today. Too much sugar. It'll rot your teeth.'

'Gwinny?' Mat said, watching from a safe distance.

'Short for Guinevere,' Gruff explained, giving the ewe's ears a scratch. 'She's a pest.'

Mat grinned. 'She looks weird, all un-fluffy like that.'

Gruff laughed. 'We sheared them today. All the Lleyn – that's what Guinevere is – and the Romney. The Romneys are the ones with lambs. The Gotlands were properly shorn in the autumn and then trimmed last month. That's what my family do, we run a wool farm and wool mill. We turn it into blankets and jumpers and things and sell them.' He carried on along the path, beach on one side and Top Field on the other. Mat walked beside him. 'That's the farm, there,' he said, pointing ahead. 'The smaller building's the farmhouse, that's where I live with Dad and Nain. The other two are barns. One's for when the sheep need to be inside, the other's got all our wool equipment in it.'

'So which one's my house?'

'That one.' Gruff pointed. 'That white cottage behind the farmhouse. It was the blacksmith's cottage, when the island still had a blacksmith.'

The cottage had belonged to the farm until Nain's parents had fallen on hard times following a terrible storm and had to sell it. If there was another storm like that one, there was nothing else to sell but the farm itself. And that would be that.

Gruff shook the thoughts out of his head.

The handcart trundled on ahead of them. Mat and Gruff were drawing level with the Sleepers now, and Gruff felt his feet slowing and a strong, quiet insistence turning him away from the land towards the sea.

The tide was out and the first of the stones was just jumping distance from the sandy shore. The swell lapped gently against the sides of the Sleepers and rolled past them to the beach, a constant hush and suck of sound.

Gruff felt the pull of the stones in the rhythm of the swell and in his heartbeat. Beside him, Mat stood transfixed.

Rosie Smalls wandered past, a bucket of beach-combed rubbish and treasures in one hand, her old, worn dungarees rolled up to her knees. She lived in one of the fishermen's cottages at the head of the beach and worked odd jobs around the island. She was kind and sensible and treated the sea with respect.

Gruff watched as Rosie stopped walking and stared towards the six sleeping stones. The bucket fell from her hand, strewing plastic, fishing tackle and a single trainer onto the beach.

Rosie took one step, two steps towards the Sleepers. Then she was walking purposefully down the slope of the beach, the firm sand thudding beneath her bare feet.

Gruff gaped.

She was going to do it. She was going to make the journey every person on this island knew they must never make.

'Rosie!' Gruff shouted. The harsh sound of his voice surprised him.

Rosie stopped and turned round. She blinked at him like a newly-woken sleepwalker. 'Gruff.' She smiled and came back up the beach towards them.

'You dropped your bucket,' Gruff said. 'Do you need a hand?'

'Oh, no, don't worry,' Rosie laughed, chucking the beach-combed things back into the bucket. 'Weird, I don't remember putting it down – must have been in a daydream! Are you Matylda? Nice to meet you! See you soon. I've got to head round to Trefynys now, or I'll be late to help Mrs Moruzzi in her garden.'

Rosie climbed up the bank of stones to the path and set off towards the fishermen's cottages. Gruff watched her go, unsettled and confused.

'One,' Mat whispered beside him. 'Two. Three, four, five, six, seven.'

'Six,' Gruff corrected, automatically. 'There's only six.'

And then he knew why what he'd seen that morning had been so wrong. His blood roared in his ears.

Mat counted again. 'Six. Oh yeah, oops!'

Gruff raked his eyes over the stones. Six, he counted, and six, and six again.

The imagined figure, the boat-mirage human.

They had been standing on a seventh.

Chapter 4

Gruff spent the rest of the walk to the farmyard explaining to himself what he'd seen. The 'person' must have been the boat and the 'seventh stone' they were standing on must have been a further trick of the light. Perhaps his brain imagined the stone in order to give the person something to stand on. Or maybe he had miscounted and there had been six like normal, and he'd just been surprised by Mat counting seven. He glanced sideways at her as they approached Blacksmith's Cottage – a small, square house with uneven stonework, lime-washed white, and windowsills painted a now-faded green. The wind turbine buzzed cheerfully away beyond the houses. John waved to them as Zosia opened the front door for the first time. 'Come on, slow coaches!' he called.

But Mat had a far-away expression and did not seem to hear him.

'Remember what I said,' Gruff muttered, as he and Mat followed the adults across the threshold. 'Don't climb on them. They're not worth it.'

Mat blinked and frowned. 'Yeah, I know.' She

looked around then, as though she had only just noticed they weren't at the beach any more.

'Welcome to our new home, Matty!' John said, grinning and putting his rucksack down on the stone-flagged floor.

Gruff looked with new eyes at the house that was familiar-unfamiliar now that elderly Mr and Mrs Pritchard had moved to their new home on the mainland. The worn blue sofa was still in front of the fireplace, but behind it now stood a new round dining table and four chairs that had arrived the week before and which Dad had set up. The floors were cold and bare without Mr and Mrs Pritchard's rag rugs, but down at the jetty Zosia had pointed out a squishy bag full of rugs and blankets waiting to make the house a home. The stone stairs on the far wall led to the two bedrooms and tiny bathroom above. In the little kitchen the flower-patterned curtains above the sink were open, showing a view of Top Field and the grey-blue sea – and the Sleepers, marching for eternity into its depths.

Gruff frowned and turned away from the window, trying to put the Sleepers and their stories out of his mind. He noticed Mat staring at the stones, the house once again forgotten.

She feels their pull, Gruff thought. Then he rolled his eyes at himself. *I don't believe that.*

They were just stories.

Just stones.

'One more load will do it!' Dad said cheerfully. 'Gruff, can you go and help James and Ffion finish packing up the shearing stuff, please?'

'And Matylda can start unpacking the kitchen things,' Zosia said. 'All right, Matylda?'

Gruff wondered if he was the only one to notice that Mat took a moment too long before nodding, as though she was having to pull herself back from some far-off place.

Dad, Zosia and John hefted the cart up again and trundled away, talking about computer programming which seemed to be something to do with Zosia and John's job. Gruff followed them into the farmyard, where they went left towards the coast path and he turned right into Bottom Field.

Gruff found James and Ffion dismantling the temporary pen as Hywel the dog watched from a comfortable patch of grass. Gruff helped them unlink the metal hurdles and carry them to the sheep barn. When the last one was stored, James and Ffion headed off home – James towards Trefynys on the other side of the island and Ffion to the fishermen's cottages at the top of the beach.

Evening was coming on and the sinking sun was

lost behind thick clouds. With Hywel at his heels, Gruff wandered over to the wool barn, where the raw fleeces were turned into soft fluff and then spun into yarn or felted into fabric. A yellow glow peeped out through the chinks in the wooden door, telling him that someone was inside. Seeing as Dad was still away with the cart, there was only one person it could be.

'Hi, Nain,' Gruff said as he let himself in. Hywel slipped past him like a black-and-white ghost and began his round of the barn, giving everything a really good sniff – the new bags of fleece, the packed, processed wool, the scouring tanks, the drying racks, the sorting table, the huge weaving loom containing half a blanket that Tim had been working on, the vats for dying cloth.

Nain was at the sorting table, her voluminous faded-blue fisherman's smock rolled up to the elbows, inspecting a fleece that she had heaved out of one of the sacks piled under the window. Sacks Gruff had filled with rolled fleeces just a few hours earlier. They bulged with promise, a harvest of wool for the future of the farm.

Nain glanced at Gruff over the top of her glasses, wispy white hair escaping from under her flat cap. 'Hm,' she said.

She had the particular frown on her face that

Gruff knew came from a day of staring at the farm's finances and trying to see hope in them.

Gruff perched on one of the tall stools at the worktable and watched Nain poke and pull the Romney fleece with expert fingers.

'*Felly?*' Nain said suddenly. So? 'Are they as bad as all that?'

'What?' Gruff replied, confused. 'Who? The New Neighbours? No, they're not bad, they're very nice.' His ears burned. What if Mat was just outside, hearing herself discussed? Then he remembered she wouldn't understand Welsh. He still didn't think they should be talking about them though.

'Of course they're nice,' Nain said, heaving the fleece to one side and pulling the next from the sack. She gave him a sly smile and he realised she was having him on. 'You've been worrying yourself over nothing. You're going to be good friends, I know it.'

Gruff smiled back. Nain was always at her sharpest when she was cheering him up.

After Mam left when Gruff was five, his spiky, kind Nain and soft-spoken, cheerful Taid had become bigger and bigger in his life. There was always work for everyone on the farm and Gruff had got used to having his wounds tended and being roundly told off for his misdemeanours by all three of his adults, whichever one happened to be nearby at the time. Then, four years ago, Taid died. Through his own numbing loss, Gruff had seen Nain turn in on herself, losing the energy to be spiky. But Gruff and Dad and Nain talked about Taid, keeping him large in their lives, and Gruff found that, although his grief would never end, it was possible for life to settle into new patterns. Over time, Nain's spikiness began to return and she became Nain once more.

Hywel padded softly across the barn and leant against Gruff's legs, bored and hoping for tea. As Gruff leant down to pat him he heard the rumble of the cart, the final load of luggage arriving in the last light of the day.

Nain gave a short, sharp sigh and drummed her fingers on the fleece she was inspecting.

'Everything okay, Nain?' Gruff asked.

Nain didn't reply, which was annoying but unsurprising. All Gruff got from Nain and Dad were accidentally-dropped hints and whispered conversations in other rooms. He wished they would just tell him how much trouble the farm was in, instead of pretending that everything was fine when it clearly wasn't.

Gruff got down from his stool and went to join Nain, but as he drew alongside she patted his shoulder, said, 'Could you put these away please, *cariad*, and get the hens in?' and hurried out of the barn. Hywel followed her, his food radar up and running. Gruff heard Dad's voice in the yard and Nain answering, and then the front door of the farmhouse closing behind them. This would be one of those conversations they didn't want him to hear.

Gruff stuffed the fleeces back into the sack and rounded up the hens as fast as he could. Then he half-ran across the packed-earth yard to the farmhouse and slipped in through the heavy oak front door. He latched it silently behind him, kicked his trainers off and tiptoed on socked feet to the closed kitchen door. Dad and Nain were talking inside, at a normal volume since they thought he was nowhere near.

'Last winter nearly finished us off,' Dad was saying. 'All those fleeces ruined from just one small roof leak.'

'Forget that,' Nain snapped. 'We can't change the past. The Lleyn and Romney fleeces are excellent this year, that's something, and the wool crew have worked so hard on what was left of the Gotland fleeces over winter. But if we can't find sellers, it's all for nothing. Boxes of jumpers and socks and blankets – what good are they to us if no one will buy?'

'If only Sali's Knits hadn't closed,' Dad said. 'If only she'd been able to find someone to take it on when she retired.'

'We need to find more outlets, more customers.'

'I know. But where do we find them? I've sent emails to everyone I can think of who might stock us, but they all have their own providers. And we lost four stockists directly because of that leak – because we didn't have products to send to them in the spring, they've found someone else and that's that.'

There was silence, then Dad sighed. 'All we can do is scrape through this year and hold on for the next. Perhaps it will get better. And the roof of the barn is fixed, so no more repeats of last year's rain damage.'

'We hope.'

'We hope,' Dad agreed.

This time the silence was so long Gruff almost pushed the door open to confront them. Then Dad spoke again and Gruff stopped with his hand still reaching for the planks of the door, not quite touching.

'Is this it, Mam? Is this our last summer on the island?'

Gruff tensed. *Don't be ridiculous,* he wanted Nain to say. *Of course this isn't our last summer! We'll make it work.*

'I don't know, Owain,' Nain sighed. 'I don't know.'

Gruff let his hand drop. He blinked rapidly, feeling suddenly as though he was watching himself from a long distance away.

He had wanted to know how bad it was. Well, now he knew. They could be off the island before they had a chance at another summer. And if they couldn't find buyers for the wool, or if anything went wrong on the farm, they might not even have another winter...

'Mair.' A voice crackled out of Dad's walkie-talkie, making Gruff jump and turn. The walkie-talkie was lying on the boot-rack, where Dad must have absent-mindedly put it down when he came in. He was always leaving it lying around. Gruff raced to it and snatched it up, ducking into the living room with its high beams and big fireplace. He shut the door as the walkie-talkie crackled again. 'Mair! Owain!'

The voice belonged to Iolo, a seventy-nine-year-old retired fisherman who knew everything about everyone, and was spectacularly good at passing his knowledge on. If Gruff could quietly deal with whatever Iolo wanted before Dad and Nain realised he was in the house, he might get back to the kitchen door fast enough to hear some more things.

'Hi, Iolo,' Gruff said, pressing the 'talk' button as he sat down on the moth-eaten sofa. 'Everything all right?'

'Gruffydd.' Iolo was breathing heavily, as though he had been running. That was surprising – Gruff had never seen Iolo move faster than a laid-back sloth.

The walkie-talkie in Gruff's hand went silent; Iolo had taken his finger off the 'talk' button. Gruff started to feel a bit disconcerted. 'Iolo?' he prompted. 'What is it?'

'The Sleepers,' Iolo said. There was a break in his voice that was nothing to do with the walkie-talkie connection. 'It's the Sleepers.'

Foreboding pattered cold, mouse-like paws up and down Gruff's spine. 'The Sleepers?'

'They're waking up. The Sleepers are waking up.'

Chapter 5

Gruff stared at the small black walkie-talkie in his hand. Iolo's words filled the room around him. *The Sleepers are waking up.*

With a finger that was suddenly trembling, Gruff pressed the 'talk' button. 'Very funny, Iolo,' he said. 'Ha-ha.'

No reply.

Gruff crossed to the front window and peered out into the dusk half-light, trying to make out the dark shapes of the Sleepers. There they were, solid and still, just discernible against the slightly lighter sky. Aligned as they had been for time immemorial.

Gruff rolled his eyes. What had he expected: to see them wandering around on long stick-legs or slithering about like armour-plated snails?

Gruff pressed the button on the walkie-talkie again. 'Hi, Iolo? You okay?'

No answer.

Now a different kind of worry took hold. Was Iolo ill? Was he seeing things? Was he even now collapsed in his tiny house with no one there to help?

Gruff clicked through the walkie-talkie channels and found Ffion's. She lived next door to Iolo.

'Ffion,' he said. 'It's Gruff. Iolo just called and he sounded strange and now he's not replying. Please could you check on him?'

There was a pause, then Ffion's voice crackled into the living room. 'Yeah, of course, boyo.'

Gruff took the walkie-talkie with him back to the kitchen, and this time he just walked straight in. Nain stopped mid-sentence and she and Dad exchanged guilty looks that a baby wouldn't have missed.

'Yeah, I know,' Gruff said shortly. 'Everything's rubbish: we're going to lose the farm and go mainland before next summer. I'm going to see Iolo. He's not making sense.'

Dad opened and shut his mouth.

Nain recovered first. 'What do you mean, he's not making sense?' she said.

Gruff put the walkie-talkie on the table. 'He told me the Sleepers are waking up and now he's not replying.'

A shadow of a smile flicked across Nain's lips. 'Story-smitten is our Iolo.'

Gruff tensed angrily. 'You're the one who's told me stories about those stones, Nain.'

'Here. It's our day to cook for him anyway.' Dad opened the oven and pulled out a dish of cottage pie. He spooned a portion into a bowl, covered it with a plate and handed it to Gruff, hardly able to meet his eyes. As Gruff left the kitchen Dad said, 'Wait! We should talk about this properly...'

'Yeah, well.' Gruff pulled his wellingtons on in the hall, not wanting to bother with the laces on his trainers, keen to be gone. 'You've not told me about it before. I'm sure you can bear a couple more hours of not telling me the truth.'

He half-ran through the dark farmyard and out onto the windy coast path. He ran as much to be away from his family as to get to Iolo. He felt a bit bad for snapping, but the more he thought about what he'd heard the angrier he got.

By the time he arrived at the Sleepers, the anger had been replaced by a complicated, intense sadness that ached in his bones.

Leaving the island would tear a part of his heart away.

Night was well fallen now. Gruff stopped and looked out to the deep, dark colours of the sandy beach and the increasingly choppy water around the jagged Sleepers. Though they had seemed to pull him earlier, he felt nothing from them now. The wind lifted his short hair and sucked greedily at the warmth of the bowl in his hands.

He should get on to Iolo. Nain hadn't seemed concerned that Iolo was spouting nonsense about the Sleepers, but she hadn't heard the catch in his voice. Besides, his tea was going cold.

And then – it was as though someone had thrown a lasso round his heart and pulled, hard, out to sea. Gruff took an unexpected giant jerking step forward, off the path, and tripped on one of the rocks in the sea bank at the head of the beach.

He fell forwards, hugging the bowl and plate to his chest. He tumbled down the stone sea bank, all elbows and knees, and thumped onto the firm sand of the beach.

He lay still, breathing shallowly and trying to work out what had happened. He had stepped forward, caused his own fall. Why on earth had he done that?

He was curled around the bowl and plate as though they contained a precious treasure rather than a portion of his Nain's bog-standard cottage pie. His cheek pressed uncomfortably against the gritty sand, but he didn't feel quite ready to move yet. He looked out to the Sleepers. The waves lapped and sucked, lapped and sucked, and in the wind the swell leapt a little higher, slapping and chopping.

With that rhythm came an urge to move. To stir himself and stand; to run to the Sleepers; to start the journey out to sea. Gruff got to his feet.

He saw a seventh stone.

On it stood a tall figure, dark and indistinct. The moon was hidden behind the gathering clouds. The figure had their back to him and wore a cloak that flapped and cracked in the wind.

Shock swept the lure of the Sleepers clean out of him. Gruff stood on trembling legs, the bowl raised like a weapon. He stared.

And blinked – and the figure and stone were gone.

Someone shouted behind him. A high, thin voice swept away on the wind. He turned and saw a small figure running along the path from the farm, stumbling on stones they could not see in the dark. Bouncing plaits gave Mat's identity away.

'Are you okay?' she shouted as she got closer. 'I came out to explore. I saw you fall…'

'I'm okay,' Gruff said. He felt unsteady, like he did when Dad woke him from a deep, vivid dream. But which was the dream and which real life? Mat seemed like an imagined sprite as she ran towards him, while the figure on the stone that was not there – they had been the most real thing he had ever known.

'What's that?' Mat panted, clutching a stitch in her side.

Gruff realised he was still brandishing Iolo's dinner. He grinned sheepishly and climbed one-handed up the sea bank. 'It's food,' he said. 'For Iolo.'

'Yol-oh?'

'He lives on his own and mostly seems to eat baked beans, so we take it in turns to cook for him.'

'That's nice.'

'Mm.' Gruff winced and flexed his elbows and his knees. He hadn't been aware before of the bumps he'd got when he'd fallen, but now he felt them all right. He looked out to the Sleepers, half-expecting to see the figure and the extra stone. Excitement licked around his fear. That had not been his imagination. And with Iolo saying stuff about the Sleepers, and Rosie acting so weirdly earlier – there was definitely something going on.

Beside him, Mat took a determined step forwards, straight off the edge of the rock bank.

Gruff's arm shot out without his conscious brain telling it to. He grabbed a handful of her jacket and jerked her backwards; she stumbled and found solid footing on the path.

'Thanks.' She laughed uncertainly. 'I guess I slipped…'

'You did exactly what I did,' Gruff said.

He turned to stare at the silent stones. Mat must have experienced that same sudden, lassoing energy that had made him step off the path.

Mat made as if to move forward again and Gruff stepped between her and the Sleepers. 'Do you want to come to Iolo's?' he asked.

'Oh,' Mat said. She looked shy and pleased. 'Yes. Thanks.'

Gruff realised he had been accidentally friendly. Maybe making friends with someone his own age wasn't so difficult.

But really, the only thought in his head when he'd suggested she came with him had been to get her away from the Sleepers. He couldn't leave Mat out here on her own, with six stones that thought they were seven, and a sea that even now leapt and grew with the strength of the wind.

Chapter 6

Iolo's house looked like it had been built by accident. It was constructed of white, lime-washed boulders heaped haphazardly on top of one another and crowned with mix-and-match stone roof tiles covered in green and black lichen. Gruff loved its untidiness. It snuggled in amongst the other fishermen's cottages at the head of the beach, short and squat against their two-storeys, higgledy-piggledy against their neat corners.

Iolo was the last fisherman to live in the fishermen's cottages, and he was retired now. Ffion lived in one. Rosie Smalls in another. Then there was Elen (who worked on the wool crew) and her baby, Bill; Tim who also worked on the wool crew and was the best at weaving; Jack and Dafydd (who worked on Evan's farm) and their baby, Rhiannon; and Hardik and Deepa (who ran a bed and breakfast from their house and a tea shop in their front garden) and their little boy, Prem. They were a close-knit community and Iolo was kept well fed despite his lack of culinary prowess.

Lights winked beyond closed curtains and the electricity turbine whirred behind the houses. Prem's bedroom window was open and he could be heard giggling loudly, probably in the midst of a tickle-attack.

It all seemed so normal and safe. With a sense of relief, Gruff realised that Ffion must have checked on Iolo and found him fine, otherwise there would be general uproar rather than this homely peace.

Gruff knocked on Iolo's front door.

They waited. The cloaked, silent figure on the ghostly stone stood tall and straight in Gruff's mind.

'Maybe he won't want me here,' Mat said suddenly. Gruff turned and looked at her, surprised by the panic in her voice.

'No, it's fine,' he said. 'Iolo loves to meet everyone. Then he loves to find out everything he can about them, and then he loves to tell everyone else.'

Gruff realised almost immediately that this might not have been the right thing to say. Mat looked like she might scarper and never come back. He thought of her returning to the farm alone past the Sleepers and said quickly, 'In a good way, I mean. He's not nasty – he just likes to know everybody. He's a nosy parker but he's really nice.'

'*Diolch yn fawr*, Gruffydd,' said a voice behind him as the door opened. 'Thank you very much!'

Gruff turned to meet Iolo, grinning. 'You know it's true, Iolo.'

'Scamp,' Iolo muttered, but he was smiling. 'No respect for your elders.'

Iolo stood stooped with his hand on the door to steady himself. His knitted wool jumper was one of the farm's, a gift from Nain the year before last. His eyes flicked appreciatively to the bowl in Gruff's hands.

'Cottage pie,' Gruff said, stepping inside.

'*Diolch* – thank you! Does it have real cottage in it?' Iolo stooped even lower when Mat crossed the threshold, giving her a little bow. 'And you must be Miss Matylda Kowalska. Welcome to Ynys Cerrig.'

'Thanks,' Mat whispered.

Gruff lifted the plate off the top of the bowl. The cottage pie was a mashed mess after his fall, but it should still taste the same. He opened the metal door in the range and popped the bowl and plate inside to warm the food up a bit. Behind him, Iolo grilled Mat on what her favourite subjects were (science: she was really looking forward to doing biology at secondary school) and whether she had any hobbies (learning about sea animals).

'Been on the beach, Gruff?' Iolo asked, suddenly.

Gruff spun round, feeling as though the question

was an accusation and he needed to defend himself – but then he looked down and saw that he was shedding sand onto the flagged stone floor of the cottage. 'Sorry,' he said.

'You went to look at them after what I said to you?' Iolo pushed, and Gruff knew now that this was a telling-off and Iolo really believed what he'd said on the walkie-talkie.

'I didn't mean to!' Gruff said. 'I was coming to see you, then I – I mean, it wasn't me, it was them – they...' He stopped, wishing he hadn't brought Mat with him. There was no way she'd believe the Sleepers maliciously lured people out to sea. She would go back to her house and laugh with her family, at him and at Iolo and all the superstitious islanders. 'I ... tripped.'

'I did too,' Mat said. 'Maybe the ground's slipping there or something? Gruff saved me from falling over the edge!'

'Interesting.' Iolo sat down heavily in his flower-patterned armchair and gestured to them to sit on the only other seats in the cottage, the two rickety wooden chairs at the table. They sat.

Gruff knew from experience that Iolo was about to tell them something important. Iolo always got comfortable when he had information to impart.

Gruff also knew that there was no rushing him.

Iolo inspected a loose thread on the cuff of his jumper. He rubbed his chin and stared off into the middle distance. He tapped a rhythm on the arm of his chair.

Gruff caught Mat's eye and they both grinned and looked quickly away, trying not to laugh.

'The Sleepers are hungry,' Iolo said, 'and the sea is waiting.'

The words settled on Gruff like cold, freshly-fallen snow.

'You know what it means, of course?' Iolo asked.

Gruff cleared his throat. 'It means … you mustn't climb on the Sleepers.'

'Sorry,' Mat said. 'What's the Sleepers? Oh, hang on, is it those stones?'

'Yeah,' Gruff said. 'It's just an old story – I told you earlier. They're meant to lure people out to sea.'

'How can a stone sleep?' she asked.

'It's just a story,' Gruff repeated, out of habit rather than conviction. He glanced at Iolo.

'It's a story we've forgotten,' Iolo said. 'There's only snippets that remain. I think you should know those snippets – both of you.' He paused. 'The Sleepers are angry. They tempt with voiceless words, luring people out to the deep, dark currents. No one returns

44

from a journey out on them. The Sleepers have been luring for as long as memory goes back – and memory on a small island like this can go back many, many centuries. The Sleepers are merciless. They are relentless. They are insatiable. Their hunger will never be satisfied. And they are strongest at the time of the Wounded Sea.'

Gruff let out a careful breath. 'The Wounded Sea festival is tomorrow,' he said.

'Yes.' Iolo did not smile. 'Yes, it is.'

'What's the Wounded Sea?' Mat asked.

'A storm,' Iolo replied. 'Around this time of year the island sometimes gets huge storms – even bigger than the winter ones, and completely out of the blue.'

'It's something to do with currents and fronts, warm air meeting cold air and stuff,' Gruff said. 'Dad explained it to me once. Anyway, we get them but the mainland doesn't. They're really isolated. When they happen, they're called *Clwyf y Môr*, the Wounded Sea.'

Mat shivered, grinning. 'Weird. Why's there a festival though?'

Iolo laughed. 'It's just an excuse for a party! Whether we have a storm or not, the island holds a festival every year on the closest Saturday to the highest June tide. The highest tide's next Tuesday, so the festival's tomorrow.'

'It's fun,' Gruff said. 'There's music and food and dancing. We raise money for the lifeboat.' The mention of food reminded him of the cottage pie and he leapt out of his chair and rescued it from the range before it was dried to a crisp.

Iolo heaved himself upright. 'You youngsters should be getting back,' he said. 'Your families will be worrying. Tell your nain and dad *diolch* for the food, Gruffydd, there's a good lad.'

'I will.'

Iolo held the door open for them and Mat went ahead to the edge of the beach. She stopped and stared down it towards the Sleepers, into a darkness filled with the sound of the sea.

Gruff paused on the threshold and looked back to Iolo.

'They pulled me,' Gruff said in Welsh. 'They pull Mat too. She doesn't seem to notice. It's like she goes into a trance.'

'I was walking round to meet the newcomers,' Iolo said, 'and as soon as I came within sight of the Sleepers … I've never felt anything like it. I've felt their lure before, of course, but today… It was like they were excited. Like they were waking up, getting stronger. I ran, Gruff. I ran back here. I ran away from a pile of rocks.'

'That was when you radioed.' Gruff remembered how breathless Iolo had sounded.

'Perhaps it's ridiculous,' Iolo muttered. 'But I've spent my life on this island, and I feel her changes.'

Gruff half-smiled. 'Nain says you're story-smitten.'

Iolo laughed. 'Your nain is the one I learnt many of my stories from. You ask her about the song that mentions the Sleepers. I'm sure there is one, but I can't remember it.'

Gruff took a deep breath. He knew what he'd seen, but even now he found it hard to believe. 'Iolo, I saw someone standing on the Sleepers today.'

Iolo grimaced. 'From the casual way you say this, I assume they got away with it and are safely back on shore?'

'It wasn't anyone from the island … I saw someone standing on a seventh stone.'

Iolo stared at him.

Gruff's heart did little leaps of excitement and trepidation.

'There are only six stones,' Iolo said.

'Yes. I know.'

Iolo shook his head, slowly. 'There is something beginning. I wish I knew what it was. You keep away from those Sleepers, Gruff. You keep away from those stones. Anything that can sleep, can wake.'

Chapter 7

Tea in the farmhouse was subdued. Dad and Nain did not pretend cheerfulness now that Gruff had overheard their conversation and knew how precarious their clutch on the business and the island was, but they were still avoiding answering his questions about the farm directly. Frustrated, Gruff gave up.

Just before he went to bed, Gruff remembered the song Iolo had mentioned. He asked Nain about it.

Nain looked relieved that the question wasn't to do with the farm. She put her newspaper down. 'It's not actually about the Sleepers,' she said. 'It's a song about a fisherman who gets saved from a storm by a morgen.'

'A what?'

'They're a bit like a mermaid. Don't interrupt, or I'll never remember the words.' Nain gave him her best cross glare and Gruff managed a smile. He waited quietly, and after a moment Nain nodded to herself and murmured, 'Yes, of course.' She closed her eyes and sang in her clear, high voice, '*Chwech Cysgwr ar y môr, pontio yw eu gwaith.*'

'Is that it?' Gruff asked, disappointed. 'It doesn't even rhyme.'

Nain opened her eyes. 'That's the only bit of the song that mentions those forsaken stones. Please don't be so rapturous in your applause.'

'Thanks, Nain.' Gruff patted Hywel and went upstairs, running the words through his head. *Six Sleepers on the sea, bridging is their work.*

Well, that was no help at all. Bridging is their work? They looked nothing like a bridge. Bridges should have two sides to them, but the Sleepers didn't lead anywhere.

Gruff got into his pyjamas. He crossed to his window and leant on the sill, looking out at the white sea foam speckling the night. He tried to imagine not being here. The thought ripped his breath from him.

He glanced across at Blacksmith's Cottage. Inside, Zosia and John and Mat were just beginning their new life on the island.

Jealousy burned. He shut the curtains and threw himself into bed.

Gruff dreamt of climbing out across the Sleepers. He jumped from rock to rock to reach the cloaked figure on the final stone, but when he reached it they were gone. The stone beneath his feet vanished and he was plunged into the merciless sea.

Gruff knocked on Mat's door at ten to nine. Zosia answered it, looking bleary-eyed and clutching a mug of coffee. 'Gruff!' she said. 'How lovely to see you. Are you looking for Matylda?'

Gruff nodded, smiling at Zosia's morning zombie impression. He had been up for two hours already, sorting fleeces with Dad, Ffion and Nain. They had removed mud, beetles, hay, bits of twig and anything else they could find before sticking the loads into the scouring tanks. This was the first stage in preparing the raw fleece to turn it into yarn or felt.

In honour of Mat being new and shearing day having gone well, Dad had given Gruff the rest of the day off, on the understanding that he would show Mat the island.

Gruff was glad Dad had suggested this. His angry jealousy of the night before seemed petty in the daylight, and he realised he did want to try and make friends with Mat. He wanted to be the one to show her the island – to show her *his* island.

'Matylda!' Zosia called up the stairs, stumbling away from the door in her slippers. 'Gruff's come to see you!'

Mat bounced down the steps, obviously on far friendlier terms with the morning than her mum was.

'Hi, Gruff!' She looked hugely excited to see him, and Gruff smiled back at her.

'Living by the sea is the best thing ever,' she told him. Then shyness caught up with her and she twisted her hands together and looked away.

'Um,' Gruff said into the awkward pause. 'Do you want to come and explore the island with me?'

Mat's eyes shone and Gruff remembered that weird moment yesterday when he had seemed to see the sea inside them. 'Yes please,' she said breathlessly.

'Dad's made sandwiches.' Gruff pointed at the rucksack on his back. 'We can be out all day, and end up at the festival.'

'What a good idea!' Zosia said, plonking herself down at the kitchen table. 'We were planning to go as well, once I've finished my top-up lifeboat training this afternoon. We'll meet you there!'

Mat and Gruff crossed the farmyard, avoiding the shadows and keeping to the warm morning sunlight. There was a brisk breeze blowing and it was shaping up to be a fine day. Gruff deliberately led Mat away from the beach and the Sleepers and towards Bottom Field. Everything he had seen and heard yesterday sat on the edge of his mind like an uncomfortable dream, and he wanted, at least for a few hours, to avoid thinking about it.

'Question,' Mat said suddenly, as they walked down Bottom Field towards the sea.

'What?'

'Did-you-want-to-do-this-or-were-you-forced?' Mat blurted.

'Oh.' Gruff was taken aback. 'I did want to do this – Dad thought it was a good idea too, but I wanted to do it anyway.' *Because this is my island, and I don't want you discovering it without me.*

'Thanks.' Mat stuffed her hands in her jacket pockets and didn't look at him. 'I've done the moving thing loads, and sometimes people have been told to be friendly when they don't want to be. I've decided I like to know right from the start.'

'Oh.' Gruff looked at her sideways. 'I've never moved. Is it hard?'

Mat shrugged. 'I've moved six times. We started in Kraków but I don't remember that; then London; then South Wales; then Mama met John and we lived in three different places in Manchester, and now we're here. Nowhere's ever really felt right. But where Mama and John are, that's what makes home.'

Gruff nodded uncertainly. He supposed that made sense. Where Dad and Nain were, that was home. But he also felt that the island was part of him, and he could not imagine life away from it.

'When did your family move here?' Mat asked, as they reached the seashore and turned right along the coast path.

'Don't know,' Gruff said. 'The earliest written record's from the sixteenth century, but we think our family's been on the island longer than that.'

Mat gaped. 'That's ages!'

Her words were a cold stab. 'We might have to move away,' Gruff said. 'The farm's in money trouble.'

He saw the stricken look on her face and didn't trust himself to say anything else. He walked ahead of her along the path, green grass to the right and rocky foreshore to the left.

At the stile across the stone wall between Bottom Field and Evan's farm, Gruff paused and waited for Mat to catch up. He felt bad for walking away, especially after what she'd said about people only pretending to be friends.

'Are you going to school with Mrs Ellis?' he asked as she climbed over the stile.

'Yes,' Mat said, smiling tentatively. 'The school's on the other side of the island, isn't it? At Trefynys?'

Gruff nodded. 'She teaches everyone, from five to fourteen. Then you have to go mainland to do GCSEs. No school this week though. Mrs Ellis's sister in Cardiff's had a baby and she's gone to visit.'

'Who else is our age?'

'We're it.'

'Wow!'

'There's a couple of teenagers who go ashore for school, but they're full of themselves and don't bother talking to anyone younger than them,' Gruff said. 'And the rest of the kids are under five.'

Mat laughed. 'That's so different from my last school!'

Gruff tried to smile but his face wouldn't co-operate. Mat was shining with an inner, growing excitement, the joy of a new chapter in her life.

This was his island. His home. Not hers.

His jealousy was an unsettling feeling and he wasn't proud of it. As they picked their way round the shore he distracted himself by telling Mat all the island stories he had learnt from Nain and Taid and Iolo.

He showed her the cove where the lifeboat broke up in 1958 and the cliff hollow where they'd rescued one of Evan's new-born calves, who'd got trapped the year before. They walked out onto the spit of land where it was said that anyone who heard singing on midsummer night would either vanish or speak in riddles for the rest of their lives.

He pointed out the island rocks that had stories told about them. With the Sleepers on his mind,

Gruff noticed them all as though for the first time. There was the selkie stone, and the wishing stone, and the rock that was meant to have been chucked there from Ireland by a giant.

In return, Mat regaled him with facts about ocean wildlife. He knew some of it, but her knowledge went much deeper than his, at least in terms of textbooks. From her ecstasy when they spotted a seal's head bobbing above the waves, he guessed she hadn't actually seen most of the animals she'd described to him in such detail.

They made slow progress, stopping to skim stones or pick up rubbish left on the rocks by the retreating sea. When Gruff spotted a fisherman's crate upside-down in a cleft, he clambered gingerly down to retrieve it. They loaded the other bottles and cartons and bits of old fishing net into it and took it in turns to carry it with them.

'There's a lot of rubbish in the sea,' Mat said quietly, as she added another bottle to the box.

Gruff nodded. 'Humans take a lot for granted.'

By the time they came round the headland and saw Trefynys, with its sturdy houses scattered around its high-walled harbour, Gruff felt that he and Mat had moved from acquaintances to friends. It was a good feeling.

Mat blinked. 'Are we here already? It's not even lunchtime!'

Gruff grinned. 'It's not a very big island! But we don't have to go straight there. Let's go inland and climb the hill, then we can cross to the other coast and go to the village that way.'

Mat turned to where he was pointing. The hill in the centre of the island rose sudden and craggy, an ancient mound that refused to be cowed by the winds and the winter storms. Scrubby bushes and bracken clung to its sides, and crowning it was another of the island's stories.

'Is that a building on top?' Mat asked as she squinted towards it.

'No, it's a massive rock,' Gruff said.

Mat laughed. 'Another bit of rock! I bet it has a story, too.'

Gruff grinned. 'Yup. It's called the Weeping Stone. It's meant to run with water when the island's in danger.'

'Creepy,' Mat said with relish. She frowned at the stone wall in front of her and the field full of black cows beyond. 'How do we get there?'

'No bulls in this field,' Gruff said. 'And no very small calves – so we should be all right. Move slowly and calmly. Also, these cows know me, and they're friendly.' He heaved the fisherman's crate onto the top of the wall and swung himself up after it. Mat stared at him, her eyes popping.

'Okay,' she said. 'I can do this.'

'It's good to be wary of cows,' Gruff said. 'But these ones are very used to people, and Evan's never had an issue with them. Promise.' He helped her climb over the wall and together they walked through the curious cows towards the Weeping Stone.

Chapter 8

'Wow,' Mat said, stopping to catch her breath as they reached the top of the steep hill. 'It's massive.'

'Yup.' Gruff looked at the Weeping Stone. He knew the whole island inside out, but this rock never failed to be a surprise whenever he saw it, as though he was not expecting it to be there.

It towered above them, three times as tall as the tops of their heads, pitted and rough and solid with a base so wide that five people could not have quite touched fingers round it. Mat ran forwards and scrambled up it like a monkey, slipping and scrabbling for foot and hand holds, but so determined that before Gruff had put the rucksack down she was standing on top of the rock, turning a slow, careful circle to see the island and sea stretched out beneath her.

'There's Trefynys,' she pointed. 'And look, there's your farm. And I can see John in our garden! And there's the fishermen's cottages. And there's the Sleepers.' She crouched and ran her hands over the rock. 'I can't find any water.'

Gruff unearthed the sandwiches and came over.

'That's because there isn't any. It's just another story. Anyway, it's only meant to weep when the island's in danger.'

'Good,' Mat said cheerfully. 'We can't be in any danger then!'

'I hope not,' Gruff muttered. He waved the wax-wrapped sandwiches at Mat. 'Catch.' He threw the parcel and Mat caught it and placed it on the rock, then bent down and stretched her hand to him as he climbed up towards her.

Gruff took Mat's hand and his world changed shape.

The sea surged in a roaring wave through Mat's fingers and up Gruff's arm; it burst in his chest and slapped against his ribcage. He could not breathe. He was drowning on dry land.

Gruff tore his hand out of Mat's and leapt back down to the ground, landing heavily and dropping to his knees. He gripped the grass and took deep, shuddering breaths. The sensation of the sea within him was gone, vanished the instant his hand left Mat's. His heart was beating much too hard, but no waves pushed against it now. Gritty soil rucked under his nails.

'Gruff?' Mat's voice seemed to come from a long way away. A second later the ground juddered beneath him as she jumped down from the rock. He felt her hand on his shoulder and flinched away, but this time the touch brought nothing. No leaping waves invading his chest.

'Gruff, are you okay?'

Gruff rocked back onto his heels and looked at Mat. She had her phone in her hand and was staring at him, wide-eyed and anxious. 'Do you want me to call your dad?'

'No,' Gruff managed to say. He pushed himself to his feet.

Mat ran to the rucksack and returned with the bottle of water. Gruff took it, careful not to let their fingers touch.

The water washed the last of his shock away and his brain began to work again.

Mat was carrying the sea inside her.

Gruff eyed Mat sideways. She saw him looking and gave him a worried grin. 'Better?'

'Yeah, sorry.' Gruff handed the bottle back to her. 'I just – I thought I was going to faint … head rush, I guess.'

They clambered back up to the top of the Weeping Stone and shared cheese sandwiches. They ate in silence, Mat's attention focussed on the long sweep of the beach and the Sleepers marching out from it and

Gruff tracing the intricate patterns of the lichen on the rock and trying to think of a way to ask Mat about the rushing waves inside her.

He finished his sandwiches and began on one of the apples Dad had packed. As he did so, he found that his finger was no longer tracing the natural sprawl of the lichen but a defined line that the lichen seemed to follow. A cut in the rock, straight enough to be made by hand. Graffiti. There were patches of graffiti all over the Weeping Stone – names, dates, initials. Gruff loved trying to decipher it.

He scratched carefully around the line, trying not to disturb the slow-growing lichen too much. He just wanted to see if this was a date and if it was older than 1647, the current record for earliest date that had been found on the Weeping Stone.

It wasn't a date; it was a letter. He had found the second downward stroke of a capital H. He put his apple core in the empty wax wrap and shifted position, squinting down at the lichen-covered surface and trying to discern the rest of the word.

The letters were all capitals. They were carefully formed: deeply cut with a knife and with extra little lines at the ends of the staves. From the handwriting of the dated graffiti Gruff had seen, he guessed whoever had cut this had done so sometime in the

1700s. Over three hundred years before, someone had painstakingly carved a word into the Weeping Stone.

HIRAETH

'What are you looking at?' Mat asked.

'Graffiti,' Gruff said. It seemed strange to say such a modern-sounding word after reading this long-ago person's letters.

'Is that an 'h'?' Mat twisted round and squinted at the rock. 'What does it say? I woz 'ere?'

Gruff laughed. 'It says *hiraeth*.'

'Is that a name?'

'No.' Gruff thought for a moment. 'It's a feeling, I guess. There isn't really an English word for it, but it's like a sense of longing and belonging and...' He paused, searching for the word Nain used to describe this. 'Yearning. For a place, usually. Or an idea of a place.'

If Gruff had to leave the island, *hiraeth* is what he would feel for it. In a way, he felt *hiraeth* for it now – an almost painful feeling of belonging that was bittersweet and buried deep in his heart. It seemed an odd choice for a piece of graffiti. Perhaps its author had had to leave the island and this was their anchor to home. The thought made him sad.

Mat fiddled with her plaits and stared out towards the Sleepers. Without looking at Gruff, she asked, 'Can you feel *hiraeth* for somewhere you've never been?'

Gruff shrugged. 'Yeah, I guess so.'

The mournful whoop of a humpback whale came from Mat's pocket and Gruff jumped. Mat laughed and answered her phone. '*Cześć*, Mama.' She slithered down the side of the Weeping Stone and paced the top of the hill, talking in what Gruff guessed must be Polish.

Gruff stuffed the wax wrap into his pocket and braced his hands on the rock to start his climb down to the ground.

Liquid trickled under his palm and ran over his fingers. Surprised, Gruff pulled his right hand away. Glistening water sprang from a jagged cleft in the rock where his hand had rested, running away down the side of the stone like a tiny river.

The stone was weeping.

No. Shut up, Gruff told himself.

There was a perfectly ordinary explanation. Springs bursting from rocks weren't that uncommon – it was just ground water, bubbling up from underneath. And if it only happened occasionally at the Weeping Stone, that would explain the legend.

It was exciting, really. He bet the water was really fresh and sweet, meeting the air here for the first time after a long, secret journey underground. He cupped his palm under the bubbling spring and sipped.

Salt danced across his tongue. Gruff spat the water back out. That wasn't fresh. It must be contaminated to taste so salty. It tasted like –

'The sea,' Gruff whispered. It tasted like brine.

In the centre of the island, at its highest point, the Weeping Stone was crying salty tears.

Water seeped out from under his trainers, springing from a different crack in the rock. Gruff jumped to his feet, flailing his arms to keep his balance. He saw another spring, and another: rivers of water gushing from the stone, the lichen turning dark beneath them. Now the whole crown of the Weeping Stone was running with the sea and Gruff half slid, half fell to the ground amid a sudden, slick waterfall.

He turned round to face the stone again and bit back a scream.

A woman was crouched at the top. Her hair was grey-silver and wild and her face was young, smudged by something dark that stained her clothes as though she had been down a chimney. Her clothes were out of a storybook: loose brown trousers, soft boots, a beige tunic tied with a belt from which hung two pairs of different-shaped metal tongs. A stained, weather-worn cloak was clasped around her neck. Her eyes burned with desperation.

She put her hand out to him and Gruff stared at her and the Weeping Stone's seething surface, grappling with fear.

'*A welwch chi fi?*' she said. Are you seeing me?

Gruff's tongue would not cooperate. He nodded.

Shock and hope flashed across the woman's face. 'Finish the sword,' she said.

'What?' Gruff had to force his mouth into the shape of the word.

The woman stretched her hand down towards him. 'Finish it, or he'll kill us all.'

Chapter 9

The woman's outstretched hand trembled. Gruff could tell she wanted him to take it, but there was no way he was going to do that. He staggered backwards a step and the woman's features twisted with such anger his fear snapped into sound. 'Mat!' he yelled, half-turning to her.

Mat was staring out at the Sleepers, still on the phone to her mum. She jumped at his shout and glanced at him, frowning.

But that was where her eyes stayed. Her gaze did not flick beyond him to the Weeping Stone. Couldn't she see the woman, the rushing waterfall?

Gruff looked back – and the woman was gone. As though she had never been there.

Relief washed over him. 'Sorry,' he mouthed to Mat, and she turned away again. Gruff walked on shaking legs to the Weeping Stone and placed his palm flat against it.

Dry as a bone.

Dry as a rock that had never even heard of the sea. But…

'You're a Sleeper,' he whispered to the Weeping Stone. 'You're *the* Sleeper. The seventh one.' And that woman – she was the figure he had seen standing on the impossible seventh stone down at the beach.

The shaking spread up from his legs and into his body so that he had to lean against the rock for support.

Should he have taken the woman's hand? What would have happened if he had?

Finish the sword. Finish it, or he'll kill us all.

Who was 'he'? What sword? The only sword on the island Gruff could think of was the one in the museum at Trefynys. And who was the woman, and what had any of this got to do with the Sleepers? Six stones on the beach and one stranded up here. Seven Sleepers in all, *saith Cysgwr.*

'Oh,' Gruff said quietly. Nain's song rearranged itself in his head. *Saith Cysgwr ar y môr, pontio yw eu gwaith.* Seven Sleepers on the sea, bridging is their work. If the six – *chwech* – was replaced with seven – *saith* – it rhymed. The song must have had seven in it once but over time the final stone was forgotten.

He still didn't know what they were bridging. And why on earth had the seventh Sleeper been moved?

As the shock faded and the shaking went away, Gruff focussed on one mystery that he could try and solve right now: Mat. He was certain that Mat had something to do with this. Mat and the sea that she carried inside her.

Mat came off the phone and turned to him, smiling. 'Mama was just checking we were okay. But then she got in an argument with herself about where we should put the stripey rug. I really don't mind, but she still told me all about the three places it could go and the reasons for and against. Thanks for rescuing me from my house today! Are you okay? Why did you shout?'

'I...' Gruff cast his eyes around for an escape route. 'I thought you'd gone too close to the edge – the earth is crumbly here.'

'Oh, okay. Thanks. It was solid where I was standing, I think.'

'Yeah,' Gruff said. 'Er ... that's why I said sorry and didn't explain. Anyway. Let's go.'

Gruff shouldered the rucksack and Mat picked up their crate full of recycling. As they headed down the hill towards the lifeboat cove and the jetty, Gruff decided on a question and leapt in. 'Do you ever feel like the sea's pulling you towards it?'

'All the time,' Mat said immediately.

Gruff glanced at her. 'Really?'

'Like I'm joined to it with a thread,' Mat said. 'I

remember feeling like that when we lived by the sea before, too.'

'Do you ever feel like it's – I don't know – inside you?' Gruff asked, but this time Mat gave him a confused look and half laughed.

'Er … no? I don't think so. What would that even feel like?'

'Never mind,' Gruff said quickly. They reached the bottom of the hill and started across Evan's second cow field, this one empty to allow the grass to rejuvenate. 'You know that story about the Sleepers luring people, tempting them? Do you feel that?'

Mat nodded. 'Yeah, definitely – it's just because they look like stepping stones, I guess. Good story, though.'

So that was that. Gruff didn't know how he could continue the conversation without telling her outright that he had felt and seen the sea inside her, and that he thought she was somehow connected to a ghostly woman and a seventh Sleeper, which was the Weeping Stone, which had wept. *Finish it, or he'll kill us all.*

He wasn't sure there was a point in any friendship when telling someone things like that wouldn't sound like pure rubbish. He said nothing more.

The Grey Seal pub at Trefynys was as busy as Gruff

had ever seen it. It was always bursting to the seams at the Wounded Sea festival. There were small children everywhere, running around and shrieking in excitement as Rosie Smalls chased them in a lawless game of tag. Eleanor and Llewelyn, the resident teenagers, sat aloof on the harbour wall and watched the frivolities from a distance. Neighbours had hung bunting between their houses and there were several open-air stalls selling homemade cakes, jams, cheese and crafty things, all in support of the lifeboat. Islanders and holidaymakers talked and laughed on the hardstanding outside the pub. From inside came the rich sound of Iolo singing a song.

As they watched the festival in full swing before them, Gruff noticed Mat close in on herself like a clam.

'Everyone's really friendly,' he said.

Mat nodded. 'There's just a lot of them,' she whispered.

'How about we go to the museum,' Gruff suggested, trying to sound as though the idea had only just occurred to him. 'No one's ever in there, and there's a porpoise skeleton.' He saw Mat pull a face. 'A very old porpoise skeleton,' he qualified. 'Like, two hundred years old. And it died of natural causes, as far as I know.'

Mat wrinkled her nose, then she laughed. 'All right. It's the closest I've been to seeing one!'

After sorting their crate of beach rubbish into the big community recycling bins near the harbour, Gruff led Mat through the crush of festival-goers outside the Grey Seal and down the gravel path to the equally crowded garden at the back. People called greetings and gave Mat welcoming looks, but Gruff waved to them without stopping. He was determined to get to the museum and he could feel the waves of self-conscious shyness emanating from Mat.

The island's museum and library were housed in what had once been the pub's pantry. Gruff unlatched the wooden door into a cool darkness and switched on the light to reveal stone walls lined with glass-topped cabinets on one side and bookshelves on the other. A couple of sad-looking stuffed animals glared from the corners and the porpoise skeleton hung from the ceiling.

'Woah,' Mat said, staring at the porpoise. 'That's amazing. Look at all those vertebrae! And it's got fingers!'

'The fingers are weird, right?' Gruff agreed. He closed the door, shutting out the hubbub in the pub garden, and crossed the room quickly to the cabinet labelled 'Medieval'.

71

There it was. Gruff put his face close to the glass and squinted at the only island sword he knew of.

'What's that?' Mat asked, appearing at his shoulder.

'Sword,' Gruff grunted, reading the label underneath. It wasn't very helpful. *Sword guard, 11th-century. Silver decoration in Hiberno-Scandinavian style. This guard was found off Trwyn y Gân and is thought to have come from an ancient wreck.*

'Doesn't look like a sword,' Mat said, leaning closer. 'Oh wait, I get it. Is that the bit that sticks out between the handle and the blade?'

'Yeah. Nothing else survived in the water, but I think the silver decoration saved this bit.'

'Silver, wow. Posh sword.'

'Useless sword,' Gruff muttered. He sighed and stood upright, glancing at the rest of the exhibits in the case. He'd been hoping to find some clue that would help him understand what the ghostly woman had been talking about. But perhaps it had nothing to do with this sword at all.

Mat wandered away from him, working her way back down the line of cabinets towards prehistory and island geology.

Gruff pulled out his phone and took a picture of the sword guard as best he could through the protective glass. Then he noted everything he could about it – its size, its materials and its decoration: the two stretch-necked birds tying themselves in knots. At last, feeling deflated, he went to join Mat.

She was standing at the geology case looking at neat rows of small rocks labelled with mind-bogglingly old dates. 'Rocks,' Gruff grinned. 'I thought you liked sea animals. There's a case of shells over there.'

'Look at that one,' Mat said, making no sign that she had heard him at all. 'It's shiny. Almost like it's wet.'

Gruff looked where she was pointing. A small lump of rock, no bigger than a fifty-pence piece, glistened darkly. Water pooled at its base.

The case was sealed. The other stones were dry.

I do not like this. 'Come on,' Gruff said, trying to keep his voice steady. 'Do you feel like meeting everyone yet?'

Mat pulled a face. 'Not really.' She turned and wandered over to the library shelves and Gruff looked back to the geology case.

The stone had moved.

It was no longer in its neat line-up. It was against the edge of the case closest to him. Behind it was a trail of glimmering water.

'Let's go down to the harbour,' Gruff squeaked, backing away from the case. He cleared his throat and tried again. 'There won't be so many people there.'

Mat turned from the bookshelf, shrugging and smiling. 'Okay.'

Gruff turned the light off with a shaking hand and cast one last glance towards the display cabinet before closing and latching the door.

Stay there, he thought. *Just stay there.*

Chapter 10

Gruff and Mat sat with their legs dangling over the edge of the harbour wall and tried to guess where a cormorant, diving for its meal in the relatively calm waters of the harbour, would pop up next. Fishing boats and a few sailing yachts bobbed at their buoys as the shadows lengthened. Back on the short road along the seafront of Trefynys, Ceri played her violin and Dave his concertina. People were beginning to form into dancing sets, encouraged by the dance caller, Helen.

Everyone was having such a good time, the unnatural things of the past twenty-four hours seemed impossible.

Gruff kept checking behind him, the stone from the museum preying on his mind.

Stones don't move.

Nain arrived in style at half past six, riding on a bale of straw on the back of Evan's electric quad bike as if she were a queen in her carriage. Gruff's dad and Mat's family weren't much later. They'd walked from the farm straight through the middle of the island, a much shorter journey than round the coast path.

After fish and chips on the harbour wall, Zosia and John led a resigned Mat away to do the new-neighbourly rounds of meeting people. Dad got talking to Evan and Nain went off to exchange rude pleasantries with Iolo.

Gruff found himself alone. He sat down on the edge of the rowing-boat-turned-flowerpot outside the pub and stared suspiciously at every stone on the road – but none of them were wet and all of them stayed as still as stones ought to.

Before long he became the centre of attention for best friends Prem and Oisín. They both adored Gruff. Playing with them usually consisted of being climbed all over, so Gruff had Prem hanging off one arm and Oisín standing on his knees and using his head as a drum when he heard Nain's voice somewhere nearby.

'It could be a matter of weeks.'

'Oh, Mair. No.' That was Iolo. He sounded heartbroken.

'The wool and clothes shop in Cardiff that normally takes an order is under threat of closure itself – not enough profits. We only heard today. If they go under, we could too.'

'Would it really be that bad?'

'If we can't find stockists, we can't afford to run

the farm. And without the farm, how could we afford to live? Owain will have to get a job on the mainland. Evan can't afford another worker.'

'But … oh, Mair.'

Suddenly, Oisín using his head as a drum was so unbearable that Gruff had to stop himself from just pushing him off. He gently disentangled Prem from his arm and lifted Oisín carefully to the ground. 'Look,' he said, pointing to tall, stringy Tim, who worked in the wool crew and was currently sitting nearby, tapping his feet to the beat of the music and blissfully unaware of imminent attack. 'I've got to go, but you know Tim, right? Tim'll play with you!'

They ran off and Gruff stood up, balling his hands into fists. A matter of weeks? How could everything fall apart so fast? He was trapped, watching the future roll inexorably towards him, carrying with it the loss of his home. The loss of Dad's home. The loss of Nain's home. The loss of the flock.

And in a painful flash, he knew what he needed to do.

He pulled his phone out of his pocket and typed a message. He read it through, and he read it through again. Then he sent it.

With it went a piece of his heart.

'Gruff!' Ffion was beside him, taking his arm and

pulling him towards the dancing. 'Come on, then! *Dawnsia!*'

Helen got them all to walk the dance so that everyone knew what to do, and then the band – which had grown to eight people now – struck up. Gruff danced with a wildness in his chest that burst out in faster spins and laughter that felt close to crying, but by the end of the dance he felt more like himself. He tried to forget the text he had sent.

Mam probably wouldn't see it tonight, anyway. She never checked her phone.

As Helen called out for people to join the next dance, Ffion disappeared and returned with a reluctant Mat. 'Here you go!' Ffion grinned, pushing Mat gently towards Gruff and leading her girlfriend Lucía into the dance.

'I don't know how to do it!' Mat said, looking panicked.

Gruff shrugged and grinned. 'Helen tells you everything. It's fun – just try one dance and see.'

'Fine,' Mat said mulishly.

She glowered her way through the walk-through of the dance, which was called *Jac y Do*. First, long lines went forward and back and crossed over. Then you did that again. Then the top couple galloped to the bottom of the set and back, cast away from each other to the bottom and made an arch which everyone else went through. Then you just did it all again, and again, until the music ran out.

'Easy, see?' Gruff grinned.

Mat crossed her eyes at him and he laughed. The music started.

By the time they had got to the top of the set Mat was laughing and bright-eyed and had completely forgotten to be embarrassed. The music lifted the dancers and twirled them through the twilight.

Gruff realised what he was about to do a split second before he took Mat's hands to gallop down and up the set. He had just enough time to take a deep breath.

He held that breath through the gallop, Mat's happiness pouring out of her in wild, crashing waves that battered Gruff's heart and lungs. He gasped for air when they parted to cast away from each other, and held his breath again to take her hands in the arch at the bottom of the set. Holding his breath helped him escape the feeling that he might drown, but as the last couple passed through the arch he pulled away from Mat with a stagger and darkness clouding his eyes, his body deprived of oxygen at just the energetic moment he needed it. Next to him, Lucía grabbed his hand as the lines went forward and back, saving him from falling.

The dance ended before Gruff and Mat reached the top of the set again. Relieved, Gruff escaped, saying he wanted some water. He was certain of one thing now, at least. No one else could feel what he felt at Mat's touch. She had held hands with other people in the dance but none of them had pulled away in surprise.

Gruff got a glass of water from Mrs O'Neill behind the bar and took it back outside, where the last edges of summer light were fading fast. He drank his water slowly, watching the next dance but not seeing it. That woman on the stone was in his mind again. Her face and clothes smudged with the black substance, the metal tongs at her belt.

Finish the sword.

'She's a blacksmith,' Gruff said out loud, surprising himself with the deduction.

She was a blacksmith. The stuff on her skin and clothes, that was soot. And that made sense of the tools at her belt, and the idea that there was a sword to finish.

Blacksmith. That was something to go on, at least.

Gruff pushed back into the pub. Iolo was holding court in the small function room off to the side, telling tales to the little ones and their families in a booming voice.

'And he came every year to the selkie stone,' Iolo said, his audience staring at him with rapt attention (apart from two-year-old Steph, who was engaged in a full-blown tantrum about chocolate brownies), 'and he shed his sealskin and walked on land as a man once more. But before the tide had turned, he would wrap his sealskin round himself and be gone with the flick of a whisker and the swish of his tail.'

Iolo fell silent long enough for everyone to realise that the story was finished, and his audience applauded. Gruff picked his way across the toddler-strewn carpet and sidled up to Iolo as he took a sip of his lemonade, preparing for his next foray into island lore.

'Iolo,' Gruff said.

'Hello, *bachgen*. No accidental trips to the beach today, I hope? You leave those Sleepers well alone, like I've been reminding every person here tonight.'

'I haven't gone to the Sleepers. But…' Gruff wanted to tell the old man everything that had happened, but there were too many ears nearby. 'Do you know any island stories with blacksmiths?' he asked.

'Blacksmiths?' Iolo repeated in surprise.

'Or swords,' Gruff added.

'Swords? Some of the heroes have swords, but there isn't a special one – not like Excalibur or

anything.' Iolo furrowed his brow. 'Blacksmith …
there's a blacksmith in the wish-granting-fish story
my nain used to tell me. I leave it out of my version
though, because it doesn't really have a purpose in the
narrative.'

'Fifteen minutes to low tide!' The call came from
outside the pub. 'Time to find a stone, everyone!
Dewch i'r traeth! Come to the beach!'

The function room erupted with excitement as
everyone started for the door. Iolo put down his glass
and went to follow, but Gruff stopped him. 'Please,
Iolo! It's important – it's about the Sleepers.'

'Really?' Iolo frowned, worried. 'I'm sorry, there's
nothing about the Sleepers in my story with the
blacksmith. In the story, just before the high tide
that washes the talking fish ashore and destroys the
village, the heroine meets a blacksmith who tells her
that danger is at hand. The blacksmith isn't mentioned
anywhere else. There's no point in him being in the
story, really, and no point in him being a blacksmith.
So I just leave that bit out. What's made you think
there's a blacksmith associated with the Sleepers?'

I've met her, Gruff wanted to say, but at that
moment Mrs O'Neill stuck her head round the door.
'Don't worry, I'll tell you later,' he said instead.

'Come along, dawdlers!' Mrs O'Neill laughed, and

Iolo popped his trilby on his head and took the arm she offered as they headed out of the pub. Gruff hung back, watching them go.

So the blacksmith foretold danger, just like the Weeping Stone did. And Gruff had seen the blacksmith, and the Weeping Stone had wept.

This was the time of year for the Wounded Sea storm, if there was to be one. Wounded Sea storms took lives.

Gruff was left alone in the empty pub, his thoughts terrible.

Chapter 11

A little further round the coast from Trefynys harbour, craggy cliffs dropped to a small pebble beach with a bubbling river running through it. Here the oldest tradition of the festival was upheld.

Gruff clambered down the earth path. Torches swung this way and that, the light bouncing off the stones and the waves. Everyone was searching for a pebble as close to the shape of the island as they could find. No one spoke. In solemn silence the tradition played itself out, year after year after century.

Gruff crouched and started to search through the pebbles. People began to switch their torches off, leaving only the light of the rising moon in the blue-black summer sky. '*Gosteg,*' Nain whispered nearby. Gruff looked up and watched her draw her arm back and throw her island pebble into the lapping water. Low tide. All around the small, packed beach, figures threw their stones into the waves. *Gosteg.* A call for calm, silence, stillness, peace. *Gosteg.*

Gruff, sifting through sun-dried pebbles, felt one

wet and slick beneath his fingers. He drew a sharp breath and picked it up, his heart hammering.

It was the stone from the museum. Same shape, same size. And it was the only wet pebble amongst all these dry ones.

In one swift movement, Gruff stood up, hissed 'Gosteg', and threw the stone as hard and as far as he could, away from him into the water.

'One,' Gruff whispered, counting slow seconds against his pounding heartbeats. 'Two. Three. Four. Five. Six. Seven.' Seven Sleepers. Seven seconds for that stone, which should not have been wet, should not have moved, to be taken by the sea.

Had he done the right thing?

That stone was following me.

On a sudden thought, Gruff touched his wet fingers to his lips. He tasted salt. Had that little piece of rock been something to do with the Weeping Stone, the seventh Sleeper?

Laughter and voices warmed the air as people turned from the sea and headed back for more food and music and dancing.

'Hi!'

Gruff jumped and turned to find Mat standing next to him, grinning from ear to ear. 'That was fun. Everyone was so serious! Your dad said we had to say goss-teg. He says it's asking the sea to be calm.'

'Yeah.' Gruff pinched his palm to bring his brain into order. 'It's an offering. That's why the stones have to look like the island, so the sea doesn't decide to take the island itself.'

An attempt to save the island from the merciless Wounded Sea storms. A shiver passed across his shoulders as he fully realised the significance of the tradition. Did it work? Would it save them? *Finish it, or he'll kill us all.*

'How long have people been doing it?'

Gruff shook his head as they climbed back up the steep path to the village road. 'No one knows. That long.'

Mat's mum bundled her away to meet the rest of the lifeboat crew. Gruff stood a little way back from the pub, watching the music and dancing strike up again but unable to walk towards it. His thoughts were full of stones that moved and blacksmiths that foretold danger. His thoughts were full of storms.

Then Gruff spotted Nain. Like him, she was alone on the edge of things, but she was not watching the party. She stood as still as a statue on the cliff path above the village, looking inland at something he could not see.

Gruff started towards her, suddenly desperate

to tell her everything. He had always told them everything, her and Dad. They were his family, his closest friends. He didn't want to deal with this on his own any more.

Gruff skirted the dancing and jogged up the cliff path to where he had seen Nain, but she was gone. He looked around and spotted her at the entrance to the barley field, leaning on the gate, staring out across the centre of the island in the direction of the farmhouse.

'Nain?' Gruff said it quietly, not wanting to scare her. She did not turn but she shifted slightly to show she had heard. Gruff went over and leaned on the rusty gate. He glanced at her and thought how fragile she seemed: paper-thin skin, tired eyes, her mouth sad and resigned.

'Your Taid and I,' Nain said softly, 'met at the festival.'

Gruff knew this story. But he didn't stop her.

'He came in on Iolo's fishing boat. Hitched a ride across to the island with a pack of his friends for the fun of it, just for a bit of dancing.'

Nain stopped. Gruff realised that her eyes were sparkling with unshed tears. His own eyes pricked.

'But that one night dancing,' Gruff said huskily, picking up Nain's story for her, 'turned him into an islander, and he hardly set foot mainland again.'

Nain's face crumpled and Gruff's own tears escaped. He wiped them away with his sleeve and searched desperately in his pockets for a tissue to give to Nain.

'Stop flapping like a panicked goose,' Nain said, and Gruff looked up to find her glistening face set into her best glare. 'I have my own hankie, thank you, and it isn't full of your snot.'

Gruff laughed and sniffed and Nain dried her eyes and nodded briskly. 'He is in the earth of the island, Gruff.'

'I know,' Gruff said. They had scattered Taid's ashes on the farm that had become his home.

'And he is everywhere I walked with him,' Nain said. She sniffed in a businesslike way, folded her handkerchief carefully and put it back in her coat pocket.

Gruff understood then what this was about. It wasn't just the festival making her remember. This was Nain fearful she was about to leave the island. Leave behind not just her home but every moment of her life. Every moment of Taid.

It had been the right thing to do, sending that text to Mam.

'You look like a grandson with something on his mind,' Nain said. 'Can your aged relative lend you some wisdom?'

Gruff's tongue was so full of words he couldn't form any of them. He shook his head. 'Maybe tomorrow.'

'Quite right, too,' Nain said, and she gave him a quick, sweet smile. 'Tonight is for dancing.'

Gruff woke three hours before high tide.

He knew this because his glow-in-the-dark alarm clock told him it was ten to two in the morning and his internal tide timetable kicked in without being asked. He turned over and closed his eyes, hoping to fall asleep again before his brain remembered all the things he had to worry about.

Too late. Images crowded Gruff's mind. The blacksmith on the Weeping Stone. The glistening lump of rock from the geology display. Nain's tears. He thought of the text he had sent to Mam. He fumbled for his phone but there was still no reply.

He stared at the ceiling, which he could see well enough to know the moon must be pretty bright outside. Why had he woken up?

A scratching noise from the floor by the open window made him jump but also answered his question. 'Hello, Mouse,' he said loudly. 'Go away, I'm trying to sleep.' Whoever had come up with the phrase 'as quiet as a mouse' had obviously never met one.

Scratch, scratch. Claws on wooden floorboards, coming closer.

'Shut up,' Gruff said, but the scratching continued. He leaned over and turned his light on to scare the mouse away.

On the floor beside his bed, glimmering at the end of a trail of water, was the stone from the geology cabinet.

Gruff bit back a yell of shock. He stayed still as a startled mouse himself, staring at the stone, waiting for it to move.

It did not move.

It's come to get me, Gruff thought wildly.

But why? Why had it moved towards him in the museum? Why had it found him on the beach? Why on earth was it in his bedroom?

Perhaps it wanted him to do something.

'What?' Gruff hissed, angry suddenly. 'I don't know what to do!'

Apart from finish the sword. And that was a pretty unhelpful instruction since he had no idea what it meant. Perhaps he should have taken the blacksmith's hand. Fear had stopped him, but now he felt only desperation to know what she wanted. If he had seen the blacksmith and the Weeping Stone had wept, the island must be in terrible danger. *Finish it, or he'll kill us all.*

The small lump of rock glinted in the light from Gruff's bedside lamp, water pooling around it on the wooden floor.

He was part of whatever was going on, however he felt about that. He may as well leap in with his eyes open.

Just like that, his decision was made. Gruff threw the duvet back and got out of bed. He dressed quickly, in jeans, long-sleeved t-shirt and wool jumper. Steeling himself, he picked the stone up. Cold salt water trickled between his fingers.

He crept downstairs and pulled his trainers on at the door before lifting the latch and slipping out. The moon shone so brightly he could almost see colour between the deep black shadows. He rounded the farmhouse and set out across the fields towards the Weeping Stone.

Brine seeped from his fist to spatter the silver-green grass.

Chapter 12

Gruff stood before the Weeping Stone and let his breathing slow after the steep climb up the hill. The small rock in his hand seemed to quiver with energy, making his fingers twitch, but maybe that was just his nerves.

All was quiet. The calm determination that had carried him across the moonlit island ebbed slowly away into uncertainty. What was he supposed to do now?

'Er...' he began, his voice sounding flat against the night. '*Helo? Gof? 'Dach chi yma?*' Hello? Blacksmith? Are you here?

Silence. Nothing moved near the Weeping Stone.

Gruff stepped towards the mass of rock, dimly grey in the moonlight. He brought his sea-soaked hand up and balanced the little wet stone on one of the jagged protrusions. A trickle of water ran down from it. Gruff stepped back and craned his head to see the top of the Weeping Stone, but there was no figure.

'Hello?' he called again. 'I want to know what's going on.'

Another gleaming trail of water sprang from the Weeping Stone, far away from where he had placed the little rock. Gruff's heart thumped in his throat. Another rivulet, and another, and then the stone burst with water like a fountain; it whispered down the sides and bubbled into the silver grass at its foot.

Gruff raised his eyes back to the top of the rock. A figure crouched there, hand held out to him.

'*A welch chi fi?*' the blacksmith said. Are you seeing me?

'*Ydw,*' Gruff said. I am. He tried to steady his breathing. 'What happens if I take your hand?'

The blacksmith stretched further towards him, clearly desperate for him to make contact. 'You cross halfway.'

Halfway? Halfway to what? The line from Nain's song about the Sleepers flashed into Gruff's mind: *bridging is their work.* Perhaps the blacksmith was on the other side of that bridge.

It was all connected but none of it made sense. But then this was what he had come here for. Answers.

He reached up and took the blacksmith's calloused hand.

The sun came out.

Gruff yelped as the ground plunged from under him, replaced by slapping blue waves. He was

93

instantly soaked up to his chest and his shoulder jolted painfully as it took his weight. The blacksmith gripped his hand tighter and hauled him up to the top of the rock. He sat there, dripping, and stared.

The Weeping Stone stood in a calm blue sea under a dazzlingly bright early-morning sky, the sun newly-risen and already hot. Behind the Weeping Stone, the six Sleepers led towards the shore where an unusually high tide hid the beach. Gruff looked automatically for the farmhouse and instead saw a cluster of round stone huts with shingle roofs.

'What's happened?' Gruff asked.

'What's important,' the blacksmith replied in a hard, determined voice, 'is what is about to happen.'

'Why is this stone in the centre of the island now?'

'An angry man moved it.' The blacksmith lay full length on the stone and plunged her arm into the water. 'Ever since then, the Sleepers have mourned the loss of their own.' She closed her eyes and fished around in the waves with her hand.

Gruff began to wonder if there were going to be any proper answers to his questions. 'Why was the man angry?'

'He believed Annwn to be wicked. He broke the bridge by moving the Seventh and now nothing can reach Dylan.'

'Who's Annwn? Who's Dylan?' Gruff snapped, feeling totally lost and more than a little annoyed.

'Annwn is a place, not a person. And you will soon see Dylan.' To his surprise, Gruff saw tears bright in her eyes. He paused, beginning to link things together.

'Is Dylan the person you said would kill us all?' he asked.

A single tear tracked through the soot on the blacksmith's cheek. 'He does not mean to,' she whispered.

She pulled her arm out of the water and stood in one swift movement. In her hand she held the hilt of a sword.

Finish the sword. Was this the one? Gruff stepped closer, fascinated. The hilt held in the blacksmith's hand was blue-silver and covered in interlacing patterns, similar to the sword in the museum. These patterns, however, writhed and wriggled as though alive. Tiny, impressionist seals and gaping whales, eel-like fish and serpentine sea-dragons, all slithering amongst tendrils of sinuous seaweed in constant movement. The hilt was formed of fluid, quivering, impossible water. Gruff reached out and tried tentatively to touch it, but his finger passed right through as though it was a hologram.

'Weird,' he breathed. He glanced up at the blacksmith. 'If you have it, can't you finish it?'

The blacksmith ignored him and crouched at the edge of the rock, taking a block-headed hammer from her belt. It seemed to be made entirely of stone, its handle finely carved with animals and plants. Something in the back of Gruff's mind missed a step. She hadn't had a hammer before, had she? Just two sets of tongs.

Gruff crouched beside her. 'Why can't you finish it?' he asked again. The blacksmith showed no sign of having heard him and Gruff had the sudden impression that she did not know he was there. He waved a hand in front of her face but she did not flinch. He sat back and shivered in his cold, wet clothes, wondering what to do now.

The blacksmith plunged the sword hilt into the water. She pulled it out and thrust it back in. She kept doing this for a while, then brought the hammer down whilst the hilt was underwater and beat the space just below the hilt. Instead of passing through the swell, the hammer connected with something hard. Gruff heard a clear, sweet note carry to him through the water, followed by another and another as the hammer beat down again.

The sun was hot and the breeze warm and Gruff slowly began to dry off as the blacksmith repeated these movements. After the first couple of rounds, he realised that the sword hilt took the same number of duckings and hits each time – seven. Seven ducks, seven heavy, hard swings with the hammer. Each blow fell a little further away from the hilt as though the blacksmith was beating out the long, broad length of an invisible, wide-bladed sword. Sweat bristled on her frowning, concentrating face. She never once looked at Gruff and he was certain now that he was only a witness to this scene. As the sword gained length and his clothes dried, tacky and salt-stained, a creeping foreboding spread through him. The sword must be nearly done now, surely? But she would not finish it; the blacksmith's command had told him that. So what would stop her?

He counted, watching the blacksmith's hands with half-unfocused eyes. Seven ducks, seven blows. One, two, three, four, five, six, seven ducks.

One, two, three, four, five, six, seven blows.

One, two, three, four, five, six, seven ducks.

One, two…

A movement broke the calm surface of the water nearby. Gruff looked towards it, expecting a seal.

It was not a seal.

A lithe, man-shaped form dipped up and down through the slight swell like a playful dolphin. The figure had two arms and two legs but Gruff saw tough webbing between the fingers and toes and skin covered in scales that flickered slate-grey and rainbow bright as the light caught them. The neat slashes of gills showed dark on his neck. There was a smile that was almost a laugh on the figure's open, interested face and Gruff could not be fearful of what he was seeing, unexpected as it was. He smiled, too, and glanced at the blacksmith. She was in the midst of the ducking and did not look up.

The man-fish dived below water, heading for the seventh Sleeper, and the blacksmith raised her hammer high for the first of the next seven ringing blows.

Gruff saw, with awful certainty, what was going to happen.

'Look out!' he shouted. He grabbed for the blacksmith's arm but she could not hear him and his hand passed through her as though she was not there. Down came her hammer, plunging through the water with the full force of her powerful swing.

Instead of one of the sweet, clear notes, that must have carried far beneath the sea and brought the smiling man to see what was happening, there came a terrible, bubbling scream of pain. Blood spread through the water.

The blacksmith's mouth pulled wide with horror. 'Dylan!'

The soft swell round the seventh Sleeper turned into sudden, jagged waves. Gruff saw the man-fish flailing and thrashing through the spray. Gruff stretched towards him, slipping on the slick surface of the stone. Beside him, the blacksmith was also reaching out desperately, but the man-fish slipped further away from them, back out into the bay. The sea howled and groaned, a storm rising from nowhere.

The man-fish was gone and the waves clawed at Gruff, dragging him towards the edge of the rock. The sea yelled and thrashed like the wounded man-fish had done, and Gruff tipped towards it.

The blacksmith grabbed his arm and pulled him back. He turned on her, angry and scared. 'You couldn't see me!' he shouted. 'You couldn't hear me! You hit him!'

Her face was running with tears. 'I can't change what's already happened.'

There was a yawing hole in Gruff's chest. 'Will he be okay?'

'No.' The blacksmith's face twisted as she held back a sob.

'He's not – he's not going to die?'

'No. He will live on and on in agony, and the island will pay.' She raised her voice to be heard above the roar of the buffeting sea. 'Finish the sword. It was forged to break waves. Finish the sword, or he'll kill us all.'

The sun was the moon and the day was night, and Gruff stood alone and sea-soaked on the bone-dry surface of the Weeping Stone.

Chapter 13

Gruff left the small pebble on the Weeping Stone and headed for home, shivering in his wet clothes. Everything he had seen and heard was bright and loud in his mind. The anguished scream and the desperate, bloodied thrashing of the man-fish played itself through again and again and Gruff could not stop his ears from the sound or blink the image away.

His thoughts stumbled in and out of focus. Dylan. The man-fish. He had swum towards the sweet, ringing note of the hammer with such open curiosity and a laugh on his face – was he really the person the blacksmith said would kill them all?

Perhaps the hammer-blow had made him so angry he wanted revenge. But the blacksmith had said that Dylan did not mean to kill.

The name the islanders gave the terrible summer storms was *Clwyf y Môr*, the Wounded Sea. Gruff thought again of that scream and the way the waves had responded as though in sympathy. If Dylan's pain was linked to the water, then perhaps his agony could become a life-threatening storm.

Halfway back to the farmhouse, the Sleepers dragged Gruff from his thoughts. He felt their pull as a keen, desperate pain in his chest, a yearning so deep and powerful he thought it would split him apart. He began to run towards them over the tussocky ground.

'No,' he gasped. He hugged his arms tightly round his chest and deliberately fell over, coming down in a patch of springy heather. He lay there, hunched up, his arms wrapped around the terrible loss and the terrible need. 'Nope. *Peidiwch.* No chance. Get lost. Shut up,' he whispered, until he could hear his own words and feel his fingers and toes and the chill of the wind on his face. Until the feeling in his chest was no longer the only one that seemed to matter.

He stood up and trudged very slowly on towards the farmhouse, visible ahead as a grey-black block in the moonlight. A dull ache inside him throbbed at every step, the Sleepers luring him still.

The wicked, angry, insatiable Sleepers, tempting people across the centuries. Sending them down to the drowning depths.

But ... Gruff found his thoughts slipping like eels into a sudden understanding. The blacksmith had said that the Sleepers mourned the loss of the seventh stone. When Taid died, his loss tore a hole in Gruff's heart. Sometimes Gruff was able to step carefully around that hole, but sometimes he fell right into it, missing Taid so badly it seemed he would never be able to climb back out.

What if the Sleepers weren't maliciously luring people? What if they were *yearning* for their seventh stone? And people felt that yearning in their own hearts and set out across the Sleepers, eventually leaping right to where the seventh should be. A bottomless hole of mourning in the arms of the sea.

Unexpected pity crept over him and Gruff veered away from the farmhouse and headed for the long, shining line of the beach. He wouldn't be long. He just wanted to see them, then he'd go home and get some sleep. He would tell Dad and Nain and Iolo about it all tomorrow, and they would know what to do.

The pull of the Sleepers was less uncomfortable now that he had stopped resisting it. His path seemed easier too, as though he was being reeled in towards the Sleepers like a fish on a line. Gruff wasn't entirely sure he wanted to be a hooked fish, but decided he was a shark who could bite himself free whenever he felt like it. Holding this thought in his mind, he stopped at the top of the sea wall, looking down at the silver beach. The fishing line pulled taut. He concentrated hard on staying in one place and did not dare raise his eyes to the Sleepers. 'I'm a shark with big teeth,' he said out loud.

The Sleepers didn't comment.

This is a bad idea, Gruff thought. It was three in the morning. No one knew he was here. He would look at the Sleepers, just for a second, and then he would go home and hide from them until he could return with Dad or Nain or Iolo or Mat. Or even Hywel the dog. Anything but on his own.

He raised his eyes.

The ragged sea was crested with fierce white. The Sleepers were great, dark shapes of mystery and temptation. The wind clutched Gruff and pushed him towards the beach, but he leant back into it and stood his ground. He'd seen them. Time to go.

A slice of darkness leapt from the third Sleeper to the fourth across a hungry gap of salt water.

Gruff tensed. Was that the blacksmith?

The figure had landed on all fours and become invisible against the rock, but now they stood and steadied themselves. Gruff saw they were not nearly tall enough to be the blacksmith. He caught his breath. 'Mat,' he whispered.

She jumped again, fourth to fifth.

She was much too small against the vast, dark sea.

'Mat!' Gruff shouted. 'Mat! Come back!' The wind stole the words from him and she did not turn.

Fear built in Gruff's chest. Mat would not stop at

the sixth stone. Dragged by the yearning pull of the Sleepers she would jump to the ghostly seventh, and the current would take her.

He felt in his pocket for his phone but it was back in his bedroom. There was no way to call for help. And if she took that final, fatal jump...

He was moving before he realised he had made the decision. Gruff half fell down the stone bank and raced across the dry, silver-moonlit sand, heading for the first of the stones.

The small figure jumped from fifth to sixth.

'Stop! Mat, stop!' he screamed, but if she heard him she did not turn. He staggered to a halt, the waves licking at his trainers. The tide was two hours off high, but already the first Sleeper was far from him. The sand beneath his feet shifted and bubbled.

'If I survive this,' Gruff said out loud, 'Nain is going to kill me.'

He waded out into the shin-high, knee-high, thigh-high water, and scrambled up the side of the first of the Sleepers. It was not as tall as the Weeping Stone, this one. Only twice his height, and a surprisingly easy climb. Gruff laughed out loud, clinging to the spray-wet surface, shocked at himself. Coming down to the beach on his own in the dark, climbing the Sleepers.

Solemn promises he'd made to Dad and Nain, broken in an instant.

He pushed himself to his feet and the wind rose around him. 'Mat!' he shouted, but still she did not turn. She was standing on the sixth stone, staring to the horizon. She seemed very far away.

The swell slopped against the Sleepers. Gruff jumped to the second, landing painfully on all fours. He sucked salt out of a cut on his thumb and leapt to the third, calling, 'Mat! Come back!'

He jumped to the fourth and stood up, preparing himself to leap again – and saw, at the end of the line of Sleepers, the seventh stone that did not exist. On it stood the blacksmith with her back to him.

He saw Mat ready herself.

'Mat!' he screamed. 'It's not there!'

Mat jumped.

The seventh Sleeper and the blacksmith vanished.

Gruff heard the beginning gulp of a cry of surprise before the waves closed softly and neatly over Mat's head.

Chapter 14

'No.' It came out as a whisper. Gruff felt as though he was choking on his own heart. 'No!' A shout this time, and he was making the two jumps to the final rock at reckless speed.

Everything he knew said he mustn't go in. Dad had taught him that since before he could walk: you don't go into a dangerous sea, not even after someone else.

But Mat can't swim. She's got no chance.

Gruff stood on the sixth Sleeper, a place he had promised Nain he would never go. His legs trembled, desperate to take the final leap into the seventh stone's gap of swirling water.

'Mat!'

The wind shrieked and threw spray into his eyes. He rubbed them and spotted something in the water, far out to his right. Was it an arm or was it seaweed?

'This is a really bad idea!' he yelled. And he jumped.

Gruff thought he knew what to expect, but the water was a horrible shock. Cold waves closed over his head. Below the choppy surface the sea pushed and pulled with unseen hands. Gruff swam upward, using calm, even strokes like Dad had taught him.

The roar of the wind and water smashed through his ears as he broke the surface. He took a breath, cold waves slapping into his mouth and leaving fiery salt on his tongue. His muscles shook and his clothes were heavy. The Sleepers were already far to his left, the current carrying him swiftly away.

The cold, dark vastness of the sea and the jagged headland, bearing down on him like a huge, hard fist, threatened to scatter his thoughts. He forced his mind back to Mat and began to front-crawl with the current, as fast as he could, trying to catch up with her. Great shudders ran through him and after the first few strokes he could hardly lift his arms or kick his legs. He pushed on, his body heavier and heavier in the water. The swell leapt around him, white-capped.

Then the swell was above him. He struggled desperately for the surface and broke it long enough to see that the headland was rushing past, out of reach, and the Irish Sea was swallowing him whole.

Down he went.

No! he screamed in his head. *I have to get to Mat.*

He was up again, spluttering mouthfuls of brine. He managed another stroke, and another, and one more, his arms and legs crying out with agony and cold and shock. He knew, in a hollow, calm place deep inside, that he had made a terrible mistake. His last mistake.

When the current sucked him down the third time, he could not find the surface.

In a fog of panic and burning lungs, he snatched useless handfuls of water. The current held him close and carried him on and out and down.

He had to breathe. He had to take a breath, but the only oxygen here was wrapped tightly in water and he mustn't, he mustn't.

He had to.

Something grabbed the back of Gruff's jumper, dragging him upwards. He lost the last of his air in the shock and choked painfully on a gasping breath of sea. Whatever had hold of him was so strong and fast that all his brain could imagine was that a seal had got him in its teeth.

He burst through the surface and took tiny hiccupping breaths around racking coughs that shook the brine from his lungs. He was still being dragged, this time along the surface of the water, out of the claws of the current. 'No!' he gasped. 'Mat! I've got to get Mat!'

There was no way a seal could be pulling him this

quickly. It must be a boat – a night fisherman who had seen him struggling. They had to go back, find Mat. Gruff twisted his head round to see who had him.

There was no boat. The person clutching his jumper was Mat.

She was swimming on her back in the water. At least, he supposed she must be swimming, to be dragging him along. But her legs were not splashing like they should have been and her free arm did not reach through the water in a back-stroke. In the one sideways glimpse Gruff managed to get, she hardly seemed to be moving at all.

Relief and confusion collided. Mat was safe.

Mat was safe.

Gruff relaxed into her grip, staring up at the sinking moon. The waves sped past him and he coughed and coughed, his throat raw.

Mat was swimming very well for someone who didn't know how to. Gruff was fairly certain even an Olympic swimmer wouldn't be able to pull someone else along at the speed of a powerboat without apparently moving their limbs. The whole thing was so weird he didn't know how to feel.

Something scraped against his back and Gruff put his hand down to find hard, compacted sand beneath his fingers. The beach. Mat dragged him up away from the waterline and released his sodden jumper. Gruff rolled over and pushed himself onto his knees.

He looked at Mat, sitting cross-legged in the moonlight in soaking wet jeans and hoodie. She gazed back at him with eyes that were wide and dark and leaping with the swell she had just saved him from.

Relief turned suddenly to anger. 'You said you couldn't swim!' His throat rasped painfully and his voice came out husky and quiet. But it was an accusation, and if he had had the energy he would have shouted it. 'I jumped in because you said you couldn't swim.'

'I know you,' Mat said.

He stared at her.

'Don't I?' she added. Gruff saw something like panic beginning to stir in her face. His anger fled and he nodded.

'Yes. I'm Gruff. Remember?'

She nodded, slowly. 'You're Gruff. I'm … Mat.'

He saw a huge shudder go through her and realised that he, too, was shaking. He somehow managed to struggle to his feet, in spite of his legs doing their best impression of badly-set jelly. He put his hand out to Mat. 'We need to get home and tell everyone what's happened. We'll freeze if we stay here. And the tide's still coming in.'

Water lapped at Mat's foot but she didn't seem to notice. She stared silently at Gruff's hand. He tried not to let his unease show in his face. Why had she forgotten him? What would he do if she refused to come with him?

Mat reached up and wrapped her fingers round his.

Gruff had not thought this through. The water hitting his ribs dragged him straight back into the nightmare. He was drowning all over again. He yanked his hand away from Mat's, gasping desperately for air. Mat sprawled backwards on the sand and Gruff instantly regretted his panic. She wasn't herself right now. He needed to look after her.

'I'm sorry!' He stumbled over to her and offered his hand again, this time holding his breath in preparation.

Mat stared and stared at the hand held out to her. Then she pushed herself to her feet without accepting his help.

She turned her back on him and walked into the waves.

'No!' Gruff lunged towards her and grabbed the sodden sleeve of her hoodie. 'Not that way. This way.' He half dragged her up the beach. Mat pulled against him and for a while it was a tug-of-war, but once they were on the path she stopped resisting and he was able to lead her away.

Gruff did not relax his grip on Mat's sleeve through the whole silent, staggering journey back to the farmhouse. He didn't know what had happened to her after she had leapt for the seventh stone and the swell had closed over her head, but he knew that he dared not let her go.

He dared not let her go, because if he did the sea would claim her.

Chapter 15

Gruff led Mat into the living room and sat her down in Nain's high-backed, winged armchair, hundred-year-old horsehair exploding out of the armrests. He fetched the small electric fire from the corner, plugged it in and switched it on. He crouched down and watched the coils burn orange-red as they warmed. He was so cold the heat was almost painful. His clothes hung heavy on him and his trainers squelched. Shudders ran through him. He was leaving a damp patch on the hearthrug, and Mat must be doing the same to the armchair. He turned to look at her. Her eyes were closed and her breath steady in sleep.

The danger of her doing a runner back to the sea seemed to have passed. Perhaps he should wake her to go home and get dry?

'Gruff?' Nain poked her head round the living room door. She flicked the light switch and Gruff squinted up at her. Her sleepy expression became wide-awake and seriously angry. 'Gruffydd! Have you been swimming?'

'Er…' Gruff got to his feet, his eyes darting towards Mat. Nain followed his gaze.

'And you took Matylda?!' she shrieked.

Mat woke up. Very few people could sleep through a bout of Furious Nain. 'What?' she said. She scratched at her neck and looked surprised to find seaweed in her hair.

'I didn't take Mat,' Gruff protested through his sandpaper-sore throat. He cast about for words, trying to decide whether Nain would believe the truth. 'And I didn't mean to go in the sea –'

'You *didn't mean* to go in the sea?' Nain repeated incredulously. 'Are you telling me you left the house in the middle of the night and *accidentally* wandered into the ocean with a girl who can't swim?'

Nain was at her sarcastic best and Gruff suddenly couldn't face the conversation. 'I'm not lying,' he snapped. 'And we're being really rude,' he added in English, 'because Mat doesn't speak Welsh. Mat,' he said, turning to her fiercely, 'you didn't miss much. Nain's just not listening to me.'

Mat stared at him. 'I don't know what I'm doing here,' she whispered. And she burst into tears.

'Gruffydd ap Owain,' Nain hissed. 'What have you done?' Pulling her threadbare dressing gown off, she swept across to Mat and wrapped her in it. 'Oh, *cariad*, you're soaked to the skin.'

Gruff stood paralysed in front of the electric fire, the warmth licking his clammy legs and his sore throat burning. Mat was sobbing. How could she not know what she was doing here? She had walked with him all the way back from the beach.

'Gruffydd,' Nain snapped. 'You go and get this poor girl's family right now.'

Dreading their reaction, Gruff did as he was told.

By the time he had brought a groggy, shocked and confused John and Zosia back to the farmhouse, Dad was awake and making tea and Nain had bundled Mat off to the bathroom for a hot shower. Zosia had an armful of clean, dry clothes and Gruff showed her where the bathroom was before retreating back downstairs.

Dad and John were clustered round the boiling kettle, frowning at it as though it was a crystal ball that could give them answers. Gruff paused at the kitchen door and wished he could run back out into the night. He wanted to explain, but Nain's outburst and Mat's tears seemed to have put a cork in his words and he could only stand in silence and wait for whatever came next.

Dad glanced up and saw him. 'Gruff!' He crossed

the kitchen in two steps and put his hands on Gruff's shoulders. 'You're soaked.'

Gruff nodded.

Dad gave him a long, quiet look. 'We're going to need to hear what happened, Gruff,' he said. 'But you don't have to tell us right now.'

Gruff nodded again. He didn't seem to be able to do anything else.

'Next!' Nain said behind them. Her bony hand gripped his shoulder and Gruff found himself swept up the stairs and into the bathroom, passing a pink-cheeked and dry-clothed Mat coming out, Zosia's arm clasped protectively round her daughter's shoulders. Mat met Gruff's eyes and said quietly, 'I did this, didn't I?'

Gruff didn't have a chance to answer. Nain was on a mission to get him warm and dry. A hot shower and a change of clothes later he found himself on the lumpy brown sofa, sandwiched between Dad and John and clutching a mug of intensely sugary tea. Warmth, relief, safety and tiredness came upon him in waves. He might have drifted into sleep if it wasn't for the daggers Nain was giving him across the room. She and Zosia sat in the two armchairs and Mat was on Zosia's lap, their arms round one another in a tangle of affection. Dad had his arm around Gruff, and Gruff leaned his head against Dad's shoulder and wished he could just close his eyes.

'You have a choice,' Nain said, breaking the tea-sipping silence. 'You either tell us what happened now, or you tell us what happened tomorrow. Either way, we're going to be sitting here for a while longer, to make sure neither of you are about to go into the sort of shock that will require an air ambulance.'

She was looking directly at Gruff as she spoke, and he felt his words shrivel again. What could he say? The whole truth and nothing but the truth? That would involve a stone that moved on its own, a trip to a distant past with a ghostly blacksmith, and jumping into the sea after Mat only to be saved by her impossibly good swimming skills.

'I…' he croaked, swallowing to try and ease the pain in his throat and still not entirely sure what words were going to come out.

'It's my fault,' Mat said, her voice muffled, her face buried in her mum's hair. She sat up and Zosia winced at the shifting weight on her legs. 'I went out on the Sleepers. Gruff told me not to. But I did. And Gruff saw me from his bedroom window and came down to stop me. But I fell in and Gruff jumped in and saved me. I'm sorry. I really am.'

Gruff frowned and Mat gave him a glare that

said *shut up*. What was she doing? First she seemed to have lost her memory, now she was giving him conspiratorial looks.

'Gruff, you should have told us instead of going down yourself,' Nain snapped. But she did not meet Gruff's eyes and he knew she was regretting jumping to conclusions.

'I'm sorry,' he said. 'I didn't think.'

Dad squeezed his shoulder gently. 'If anything like that happens again, you tell us, all right?' he said. Gruff nodded.

'Thank goodness you were there,' John said. 'Mat can't swim. Did you know that?'

'We sort of saved each other,' Gruff mumbled, heat climbing up his neck and taking his ears prisoner.

Slowly the adults relaxed and began to smile and chat about swimming lessons and sea safety. Gruff's exhausted muscles ticked and jumped and his mind was equally agitated. Mat had half-lied and half-truthed. She had glared at him not to contradict her. Why? Did she remember after all? Did she remember swimming like a fish?

And at last, his brain was back in gear.

Gruff had seen someone else swim like that. He had seen them that very night, under bright sunlight and hundreds of years in the past.

119

Dylan. The man-fish the blacksmith had struck, who had torn the waves into fury. He had swum in the same way Mat had, hardly flicking his legs or hands, sinuous and powerful and sleek.

Gruff stared at Mat and forgot about his tea. He watched her sip from her own mug and smile at something her mum said, and he watched her come over to the sofa and receive a hug from John, and sit cross-legged on the floor and allow her eyelids to droop as the adults talked. He tried to imagine her being like that man-fish: scaled and impossible, a creature of the sea.

Surely she couldn't be? She was clearly human. Dylan – well, he'd been quite a lot fish.

Gruff was too tired for this. His thoughts became steadily muzzier and his eyes closed of their own accord.

'Gruff?' Dad shook his shoulder and Gruff swam groggily out of half-sleep. Everyone was standing up. Mat looked as sleep-confused as him, her hand clasped in John's. The new neighbours were on their way out, and Gruff stumbled to the front door with the leaving party.

As the adults said their last pleasantries, Mat tugged on Gruff's jumper. He looked up to see that her eyes were clear. No leaping waves and no tiredness either. She was serious and awake.

'Gruff, you've got to tell me what happened,' she whispered. 'I don't know what happened.'

Zosia and John set off across the yard, Mat hanging back though her hand was still in John's. 'Gruff!' she whispered, an edge of panic in her voice.

Gruff nodded. 'Okay,' he croaked.

Mat turned away and leaned into John's arm, letting him lead her round the corner of the farmhouse and out of sight. Gruff watched them go.

So that was it. She didn't know what had happened.

There were two Mats: one could not swim and one swam like a fish. And the one who could not swim did not remember the Mat that had walked straight into the waves without a backward glance.

Chapter 16

Gruff woke at half past nine with a raging sore throat. He checked his phone. No reply from Mam. His heart thudded with relief and disappointment.

Unable to get back to sleep and unwilling to lie there with only his own thoughts for company, he got out of bed and found the small, sea-wet rock he had left on the Weeping Stone making a little puddle on the rug.

'Oh,' he croaked. 'Hello.'

It didn't scare him anymore. He got dressed and slipped it into the pocket of his jeans, letting its weight be a reminder of the truth of everything that had happened the night before. He wondered whether to wrap it in something to stop it soaking through the material but it settled for just making a small damp patch, which was bearable.

On the kitchen table he found a note from Dad, along with a jar of honey and a lemon. *We're at the wool barn. Only come if you feel up to it. If your throat's bad, try honey and lemon. Love Dad.*

Going to the wool barn sounded like a good idea. Mat

had looked desperate to hear what had happened, but he wasn't ready to think about it all again yet. He wanted to remember what reality was first. And he wanted to be doing something for the farm, instead of just worrying about its money problems from a distance. Mat could come and find him when she was ready.

He made porridge for breakfast. It was easier on his throat than toast.

*

The day was windy but the sun was warm. The top half of the barn door was held back by twine, the bottom half closed to keep out the chickens scratching and pecking in the yard. Laughter and crackly-radio pop music drifted towards Gruff as he approached, and he unlatched the door to a chorus of welcome. Nain and Elen (with baby Bill in his sling) were hand-picking the last of the raw fleeces while Dad laid newly-scoured fleeces to dry on the racks. Tim sat at the loom, his earrings winking in the sunlight streaming through the windows. He was weaving a blanket with the last of the Gotland yarn from the fleeces shorn in the autumn. The Gotland winter fleeces, shorn in the spring, were on the other side of the island, being felted by Mrs Moruzzi at her house.

Gruff set himself up at the other end of the table to Nain and Elen and sorted the newly-scoured and dried fleeces into different lengths of fibre that would be put through the carding machine and turned into soft, fluffy material to be spun or felted. The team talked and laughed around him and the radio crackled in the background. Old Hywel was stretched out in a patch of sunlight on the floor, fast asleep. A quiet contentment settled on Gruff, and everything he'd been worrying about seemed to fade. This was home. This was right.

At twelve o'clock, Mat's head peered over the half-door of the barn. Dad spotted her first and waved. 'Come in, Mat!'

She unlatched the door and three hens threw themselves past her feet, overjoyed to be somewhere they weren't normally allowed and which they therefore naturally assumed was full of food and other excitements. After the hens had been shooed out and Mat had stopped apologising, she was given a tour of the wool processes. She then helped Nain and Elen pick over two fleeces until lunch.

Gruff and Mat escaped after sandwiches in the farmhouse kitchen and sat on the top rung of the gate between the yard and Top Field. Gruff wondered where to begin, but Mat began for him. 'Can you feel them?' she asked.

Gruff followed her gaze out to the Sleepers and felt that insistent tug. 'Yes.'

'I'm not imagining it,' she said. 'Is it magic?'

'I don't know.' *Magic*. What a strange word. He supposed that was what all these things were. All these impossible things.

'I remember going to the Sleepers last night,' Mat said quietly. 'I couldn't sleep, and I was watching them from my window. I wanted to see them closer, so I went to the beach. The first stone was so close. I waded out and climbed it. I was going to go to the end and then come back. I promise that's all I was going to do. But when I jumped onto the last stone it just … it just disappeared.' She stopped. 'I know that sounds really weird. But that's why I fell in the water.' She paused and looked down at her knees. 'I was drowning. And then I woke up in your house.'

A meadow pipit chittered on the stone wall to their left. Gruff wondered where to begin. 'Does your throat hurt?' he asked.

Mat glared at him. 'What? Why does that matter? You said you'd tell me what happened, so just tell me!'

Taken aback by her spurt of anger, Gruff hesitated. 'It's important, I promise. Just answer and I'll tell you what happened.'

'My throat's fine. My neck's itchy though. I think a

jellyfish stung me or something. Your throat sounds bad.'

'Yeah.' Gruff nodded. 'Exactly. It's the salt water and the choking. If you were close to drowning you should be feeling like this too.'

'Well, I'm sorry,' Mat said grumpily. 'I'm sorry my throat's fine.'

'That's not what I mean.' Gruff closed his eyes and put his thoughts in order, stringing them into sentences. 'I jumped into the sea after you, and the current took me. I thought that was it. I thought I wouldn't find you and we would both drown. Then you grabbed me and swam me to shore. You saved me; I didn't save you.'

Mat stared at him open-mouthed. 'What?'

'And then,' Gruff said, 'you tried to walk back into the sea and I had to practically drag you home.'

She shook her head. '*What?*'

'That's what happened.'

Mat jumped down into Top Field and walked away.

'Mat?' Gruff called, but she didn't turn. 'Mat!' He followed and fell into step beside her, but still she wouldn't look at him.

'Why are you lying to me?' she hissed, in a voice that hiccoughed with suppressed tears. 'You're just lying!'

'I'm not.' He cast about for a way to convince her.

'That's why your throat's important. It's proof – you must have been okay in the water, better than me.'

Mat turned to face him. 'I. Can't. Swim.'

'Yes, you can,' he said. 'You swam like a fish. Like, really. Like a fish. Not like a human.'

Her lip was trembling now. 'Why are you being so mean? Is it because I'm new?'

'Please, Mat!' Gruff could feel the thin threads of their new friendship snapping. Mat was part of whatever was happening and he wanted her to see it. He needed her to see it. 'You're the only one who's going to believe me! Except maybe Iolo. And no one listens to Iolo's stories. I saw that last stone disappear too. It's the seventh Sleeper, and it's not really there. That's why you couldn't land on it. It's the Weeping Stone.'

'You're not making sense.'

'That's because I'm trying to tell it too fast.' Gruff scrubbed one hand through his short hair. 'Please. Just let me tell you what I've seen. Let me tell you beginning to end, and don't judge until you've heard it all. And if you think I'm lying, fine. Think that, and stop talking to me and stop being my friend if you want. But please listen to me first.'

Mat glared at him. A nearby herring gull tipped its head back and laughed into the sky.

'Okay,' she said at last. 'Tell me.'

Chapter 17

'So,' Mat said, when Gruff had finished telling her everything – the Weeping Stone, the blacksmith, the fateful, far-off day when a hammer had struck Dylan a near-deadly blow. 'So, I'm a fish-person?'

'Um…' Gruff shrugged. 'I've no idea.'

'Like a *syrenka*. A mermaid.'

'Dylan didn't have a tail. I don't know what he was.'

'How can I be a fish-person and not know it?' she asked, staring at her hands as if expecting them to sprout scales. She shuddered. 'Weird. Really, really weird.'

'Thanks for saving my life,' Gruff said.

Mat half-laughed and rubbed her neck. 'Thanks for stopping me from walking back into the sea.'

They sat on the grass of Top Field, their backs to the stone wall. Curious teenage lambs clustered nearby, nudging one another forward and prancing away in delighted fear if either Gruff or Mat made any sudden movements. The grinding crunch of busily chewing sheep mingled with the cries of gulls above. Gruff took a deep breath and relaxed against the wall. Mat believed him. He wasn't alone.

'So Dylan's going to kill us all?' Mat asked bluntly.

It sounded horribly real coming from someone else's mouth.

'The blacksmith says he will if we don't finish making the sword she was making when she hit him,' Gruff said. 'But I don't even know where it is.'

Mat pulled up a handful of grass and let the wind scatter it from her fingers. 'You said the blacksmith dropped it,' she said. 'If it's made of water it won't have just sunk; the sea will have carried it away. We need to work out where the currents took it.'

'Hundreds of years ago,' Gruff pointed out.

'So? It wasn't far from land when she dropped it, it'll have come back in. Just like rubbish on beaches. I was reading about it the other week, how some places get more rubbish because of the currents. If you drop something in at the end of the Sleepers, where would it go?'

Her determination kindled a spark of hope in Gruff's chest. 'The current took me to the right,' he said. 'I was being pulled past the end of the beach, past the headland. I'd have ended up out in the open water … but then … I don't know.'

'We need sea charts or something,' Mat said.

Gruff grinned. 'Let's go see Iolo.' He leapt to his

feet, adrenalin spiking through him. Maybe there was a chance they could do this.

They arrived outside Iolo's house just as Iolo himself appeared from the other direction, ambling back from his overnight stay in Trefynys after the festivities. He waved at them, but winced when they both started talking at once. 'My ears are a little sensitive today,' he said. 'Let's get inside and sit down, and let's all talk in nice, quiet voices.'

They told him everything. Iolo frowned at his knees and listened intently. At last he got up and fetched a large, flat file like the ones Tim carried his paintings in to keep them safe. Inside were lots of clear pockets, and in each pocket was a map. Iolo flicked through, pulled one of the maps out and spread it on the table.

'You need to tell your nain about this, you know,' he said to Gruff.

Gruff thought of Nain's anger when he'd been unable to explain what had happened last night and her disbelieving smile when he had told her Iolo thought the Sleepers were waking up. 'She won't believe me,' he said sadly.

'She will. Your dad too. They know these things, even if they don't talk about them. Even if they try to convince themselves they're not real. Your nain saw the stone weep when she was a child.'

Gruff stared. 'What?'

'Just before the storm that took half the farm with it. And half the flock. And almost her own da. That was when they had to sell Blacksmith's Cottage, or they would have been forced mainland. They had little enough money before it happened.'

'Half the flock?' Gruff whispered. His heart panged in sympathy. He couldn't imagine losing the sheep like that. It was bad enough when just one of them got poorly and couldn't be saved. Half the flock in one go? 'She never told me.'

'You ask her,' Iolo insisted. 'Tell her you saw the stone weep. She'll know what that means. We have to be prepared.'

Gruff looked out of the window at the sunny summer's day. 'So it definitely means a storm?'

'Is Dylan really going to come for us?' Mat asked in a very small voice.

'Not if we finish making the sword for the blacksmith,' Gruff replied, wishing he felt as certain as he sounded.

'Right.' Iolo spread his thick, calloused fingers over the map on the table. 'If you dropped something in off the end of the Sleepers, it would go this way...' He traced the current that had swept Gruff along the night before. 'Out beyond the headland. And then...'

He followed the complex lines, back in towards the island, and tapped his finger on the boulder-strewn shoreline where the lifeboat had come to grief in 1958. 'Here. It should be here.'

'Hopefully,' Gruff muttered.

'It *will* be.' Mat turned to him, her face set. 'It has to be. We'll find it.'

'I'll put the storm alert out on the walkie-talkie,' Iolo said. 'Everyone on the island will be warned before tonight.'

'How long do we have?' Mat asked.

Iolo shook his head. 'We can't know. It's always the same with the Wounded Sea storms – they're impossible to predict.'

Mat stood up. 'We'd better get on with it, then.'

It was a silent journey. Gruff and Mat walked the shortest route, crossing Top Field diagonally and then Evan's cow field before clambering over the wall onto the cliff path at the head of the cove. Gruff's thoughts pounded with the revelation about Nain. She had always told him the old stories but he hadn't realised she had experienced them herself. And to have lost half the flock like that – how horrible it would be to lose Guinevere and Baa-bara and Dave and Cai and the rest of them, and all of the mischievous lambs. Poor Nain.

They climbed down into the cove and stared at the jumble of rocks. Some of the boulders were bigger than a car, some as small as their scrunched-up fists. The tide was on its way in, but the steep drop into deep water here meant that all the cove's boulders would be above water for a while longer.

'What did it look like again?' Mat asked, breaking their silence.

'It was a sword hilt,' Gruff said. 'The bit you hold, and the bit that protects your knuckles. It had fish and whales and seals and a sea dragon all knotted round each other like carvings, but they were moving. It looked like it was made of water, but she held it like it was solid.'

Without another word, Mat set off for the right hand side of the cove, picking her way through the boulders. Gruff watched her go, the impossibility of finding something made from water in a watery place threatening to overwhelm him. Then he turned and climbed through the rocks to his left and began to search.

He worked his way up and down the cove in tight, thorough passes. He searched round every rock, moving the smaller ones and peering into the nooks and crannies between those too big to shift. He found an angry crab who had a really good go at removing two of his fingers, a broken plastic buoy washed in from a fishing net, three plastic bottles, a metal oil drum and a lump of whale bone, smoothed by years at sea. Nothing glinted at him, blue-silver and watery.

He glanced round occasionally to see Mat inching ever closer towards him, a little pile of treasure and rubbish growing on a flat-topped stone she had chosen for the purpose. Plastic bottles, crisp packets, a toy metal car, a cracked bucket shaped like a sandcastle.

By the time they met in the middle, the sun had moved an hour further on in the sky. The wind blustered and they huddled behind one of the larger rocks to keep away from its cold fingers.

'That didn't work,' Gruff said unnecessarily.

'It should be here, though,' Mat groaned. She put the end of one of her plaits in her mouth and chewed it. 'If she dropped it off the end of the seventh Sleeper, this is where it would have come.'

Gruff shook his head, voicing the worry that had been building inside him with every fruitless minute. 'It might have come here to start with, but there must have been hundreds of storms since then. It could have been washed out again, into a different current. It could be anywhere round the island – or Ireland, or Wales, or at the bottom of the sea.'

'It's made of water, so it can't have sunk to the

bottom of the sea,' Mat insisted. 'I bet it didn't go far from here, even with a storm. Let's try the next cove round.'

'It's made of water,' Gruff repeated, a thought blossoming neatly in his mind.

Mat got to her feet. 'I'm going to the next cove.'

'No, wait,' he said. 'I think I know where it is.'

She caught the excitement in his voice and grinned. 'Really?'

'Really.'

Gruff ran across the uneven stones to the edge of the water and found himself a nice flat boulder that wouldn't try and poke a hole through him. He lay on his front, rolled his jumper up above the elbow and plunged his arm into the water. Goosebumps prickled to life and he shuddered, but he didn't pull his hand back out.

Mat crouched beside him, chewing on her plait again. 'What're you doing?'

'I don't know, really.' Gruff closed his eyes and tried to remember what he had seen last night. 'The blacksmith put her hand in the sea and felt around for a bit, then she pulled out the hilt. What if it was only there because she was looking for it? What if it could be anywhere in the sea, and you just have to want it?'

In his mind's eye he saw the blacksmith again,

fishing around in the water as though she was feeling for something that she knew was there, but wasn't sure of the exact place. Gruff moved his hand about in the water, imagining the hilt, seeing it as he had seen it the night before: blue-silver, squirming sea beasts, simultaneously solid and insubstantial.

And there it was in his hand. He felt it firm in his palm, a resistance of water that he could wrap his fingers around.

Heart soaring with victory, he opened his eyes and began to pull his arm out of the sea. He saw the form of the hilt through the rippling water as he brought it up towards the sunlight, and Mat saw it too and whooped in excitement.

Gruff's hand broke the surface and the hilt shattered into a million droplets, his numb, wet fingers closing on nothing.

'No!' he yelped. He threw himself down on the boulder and plunged his arm back in.

It happened again. Gruff felt for the hilt and there it was, solid in his hand, but it returned to fluid water as soon as it met the air. He tried a third time, He tried a third time, but still he couldn't bring it out of the sea. He sat back and scrubbed his wet, freezing arm with the sleeve of his jumper. 'I can't get it,' he said flatly. 'That's really annoying.' He brightened. 'But I did find it!'

'Can I try?' Mat asked.

Gruff shrugged. 'Yeah, if you want.'

Mat rolled the sleeve of her hoodie up and chose her own boulder, a little way away. She lay full-length and stuck her arm in the sea, letting out a small squeak at the cold. Gruff watched her, flexing his fingers to try and get some life back into them. After a few seconds he saw a tremor of excitement run through her and knew she must have felt the hilt form itself in her hand. She pulled herself into a kneeling position, drawing her arm up and out of the sea. Gruff waited for the moment when the hilt would reach the surface and burst into water droplets.

But Mat's hand was free of the water and she was standing up and turning to face him, her pale, dripping arm lifted in triumph. Glinting in her grasp, sea creatures curled and shifted through the hilt of the blacksmith's sword.

Chapter 18

Mat's face shone with excitement. 'I did it!' she squealed, waving the hilt above her head.

Gruff forced a grin. 'Well done!' he called. He should be happy – he was happy. But he was annoyed that it hadn't been him. Why could she pull the sword out when he just ended up with a fistful of water?

Mat had obviously asked herself the same question. 'Maybe it's because I'm a fish-person?' she suggested as he walked over to her.

'Yeah,' Gruff said, trying to sound enthusiastic but knowing he probably just sounded jealous. Mat was special, so she was the one who could hold the sword, and she would be the one to save the island. He was not special. He was useless. He couldn't do anything to save the island, or his family. He couldn't do anything to save the farm.

Maybe the island didn't want him.

Gruff pulled his phone out of his pocket without really meaning to and checked the messages. Nothing.

Mat laughed. 'I can't believe you're checking your phone. Look, real life, right in front of you!'

Gruff shoved his phone back in his pocket and scowled at her. 'You don't know what my real life is.'

Mat's face fell. Suddenly she was as shy and unsure as she had been when she first stepped off the boat. The silence stretched.

'So, we've got it,' she said eventually, in a small voice. 'What now?'

'We need to finish it,' Gruff replied. He was already regretting snapping but he didn't know how to go back and make it better. He put a careful hand out and felt in the air just below the hilt that Mat held in front of her. His hand passed through without resistance, but when he brought his fingers away they were wet.

'Woah.' Mat's eyes were wide. She put her own hand out to copy him, but Gruff batted her fingers away, getting a brief pulse of waves from the touch.

'Careful!'

'What?' Mat hunched her shoulders protectively.

'If I can't hold the hilt, maybe I can't feel the blade properly. If you *can* hold it, then maybe the blade could cut you. Just be careful.'

'Oh.' Her shoulders relaxed. 'Fair. Thanks.' She put her hand out more slowly, and brought her index finger down onto the space just below the hilt, what would be the flat of the blade if there was one.

139

There was. Her finger stopped in thin air, and she tapped experimentally. A soft, musical ringing accompanied the taps, a pale reflection of what Gruff had heard when the blacksmith had hammered the blade. Gruff grinned despite himself. This was pretty great, even if he couldn't touch it himself. It was genuine, actual magic.

Mat, her mouth open with amazement, tapped slowly down the length of the invisible blade until the struck notes overlapped into a sound that was as solid and insubstantial as the sword itself. And then, just before she reached the length of her arm, Mat tapped and her finger met only air.

'That's where it happened,' Gruff said. He remembered the sickening moment when the blacksmith's hammer had met Dylan instead of the sword, turning the man-fish's curious, laughing smile to agony and anger.

Mat retraced her steps back towards the hilt, moving her taps from side to side across the blade. 'I think it's nearly finished,' she said. 'The blade's as wide as the length of my finger at the hilt, but it's much narrower where it stops – so it must be nearly at the point. Does that make sense?'

'Yes.' Gruff put his hand out again and swept it through the wet air, his fingers dripping seawater. 'It's nearly done. We need to do the last bit. You need to. I can't touch it.'

'*We*,' Mat said firmly. 'Don't we need a hammer as well as the sword, though?'

'Oh. Good point.' Gruff had been so focussed on finding the sword, he hadn't thought about how to actually finish making it. His heart sank. 'We've got hammers at home but I bet we need the blacksmith's one. She didn't give it to me.'

'She didn't give you the sword, either,' Mat pointed out. 'Maybe the ones she has are like ghost versions.'

'Yeah, I guess,' Gruff said, thinking this through. 'And I've just remembered, she didn't have the hammer on her belt until she started making the sword. It just appeared, when she couldn't hear me or see me. Maybe she doesn't have it any more.'

'What about the museum?'

'No. There're definitely no hammers there.' He thought for a moment. Iolo had only known one story with a blacksmith in it, but maybe Nain knew more, hidden in her deep store of memories. 'Nain,' he said. 'Let's go talk to Nain.'

They walked back to the farmhouse, Mat holding the sword hilt carefully at her side. 'I wonder if I *could* cut myself on it,' she said conversationally as they climbed the gate out of Evan's field.

'Don't try.'

'I won't.' Mat gently brought the hilt down towards the grass at her feet.

Gruff looked at her. 'What are you doing?'

'Just seeing if it'll cut – oh.'

The hilt was almost touching the ground now, but no cut had appeared. Instead, a pool of water trickled and spread.

Gruff stared, fascinated. 'Maybe it's because it isn't finished yet?'

Mat tapped the empty space below the hilt and the note rang out again. 'I'm not sure this can get any weirder.'

Nain was sitting in the little patch of scrubby grass and wildflowers at the back of the farmhouse. It was a garden of sorts, the sheep kept out by tumbledown stone walls. Gruff knew Mam had battled with it when he was young, planting flowers that never seemed to do well in the salt-blown island air. It was one of the things he remembered her being frustrated with, a thing that made her sad. Now the garden grew as it wished to, hardy flowers and stony soil.

Nain had set herself up with her canvas chair and the rickety folding table covered in papers, cardboard folders and the laptop. The ferocious way she was scowling at it all could mean only one thing.

'Oh dear,' Gruff said. 'She's doing the accounts.'

'Is now a bad time?' Mat asked.

Gruff shrugged. 'We might as well just go for it. But if she snaps, don't take it personally, okay?'

He noticed a tremble in Mat's sword arm. 'Are you all right? Is it heavy?'

'Not really. It's hard to carry, though.' Mat sucked her top lip, looking for words. 'It feels like it's … excited? *Ready*. Like a cat, all wound up before it jumps.'

Gruff reached out his hand, desperate to feel what she described, but he let his arm drop again. His fingers would just pass through. He swallowed his disappointment and led the way through the wooden gate.

Nain did not look up as they approached and Gruff guessed she'd seen them coming from afar. She squinted at the screen in front of her, tsking quietly. Gruff saw the columns of a spreadsheet. 'Er … Nain?' he tried.

'No,' Nain said. 'Another time.'

Gruff folded his arms and stood his ground. Nain and Dad had put him off far too many times recently. They'd used up their share of conversation escapes. 'Mat just pulled a magical sword out of the sea, and yesterday I saw the blacksmith on the Weeping Stone and it wept,' he said calmly.

143

'Hm,' Nain said, though whether at the spreadsheet or at him, Gruff couldn't tell.

'All right,' he said, and he led Mat to a driftwood log used as a garden bench and sat down. Mat let her hand rest on the log beside her but didn't relinquish her hold on the hilt.

'What now?' Mat asked.

'Give her a second,' Gruff said. 'She gets really focused in on stuff. We just have to wait for her to hear what I said.'

Sure enough, after half a minute of Gruff and Mat watching a honey bee feasting amongst the clover, Nain's sharp voice cut the calm. '*What?!*'

She came stumbling across the grass, bringing her folding chair with her. She plonked herself down in it and regarded them both through narrowed eyes. 'You do not joke about the Weeping Stone, Gruffydd,' she said, in a quiet, dangerous voice.

'I wasn't joking.'

Fear swept across Nain's face. For the first time in his life, Gruff really understood that his grandmother had once been a child.

'When I was seven,' Nain said softly, 'I saw that stone weep. Within the week, a storm had taken most of the outbuildings and half of our flock. My da, he almost died trying to save them. He swallowed so much sea. His lungs were never the same.' She paused, twisting her gnarled fingers together. 'We nearly lost the farm.'

'Iolo said that's when you sold Blacksmith's Cottage,' Gruff said.

Nain looked at him sharply. 'He told you that?'

'Because I told him about the Weeping Stone.'

Nain was silent. 'You didn't feel able to tell me.'

Gruff squirmed. 'I didn't know if you'd believe me, and you and Dad are so…' He searched for the word.

'Preoccupied?' Nain finished for him. 'Evasive? I know we've not been answering your questions about the farm, *bach*. To protect you.'

'I don't need protecting,' Gruff muttered.

'I wouldn't be so sure.' A shiver went across Nain's shoulders. 'If that stone has wept we will all need protection before the week is out.'

Chapter 19

Gruff looked at Nain's hands, clasping and unclasping. She seemed defeated already, as though there was nothing to be done – and coming from his brave, determined Nain, who had looked after him and scolded him and teased him and always been the strong one, that scared him. But if there really was no hope, why had the blacksmith spoken to him?

'I met the blacksmith, Nain,' he began, 'and she told me – us – to finish the sword. I saw her hit Dylan with her hammer, but it was an accident. And now Mat's pulled the sword out of the sea, so all we need is the hammer, and we can finish it. And maybe that'll put things right.'

Though I don't see how, he thought. How would finishing the sword stop the storm?

Nain looked at him with slightly unfocussed eyes, still dwelling on her own memories. Slowly he saw her come back to herself, her fear giving way to bafflement. 'Would you like to try a different language?' she said at last. 'I'm not sure I know the one you're speaking.'

Mat grinned and held up the sword hilt still

clutched in her left hand. Nain's eyes grew big and round behind her thick glasses and she reached towards it.

'Careful!' Gruff and Mat yelped as one, but Nain's fingers went straight through and came away wet. Gruff smiled a little. It wasn't only him who couldn't touch it, then.

'Explain,' Nain said softly.

When they had finished, Nain sat back in her chair and looked up at the sky, tapping the tip of her nose. 'Well,' she murmured, after a while. 'Well.'

'All right then,' she said, looking back at them, and Gruff saw a gleam in her eyes that he knew was hope. 'There hasn't been a blacksmith on the island for over a hundred years, but the last one was on this farm. Start in the toolshed. We've kept all great-great-great-great-uncle Aled's tools, so if he had the hammer that's where it would be.'

Nain returned to her accounts with new vigour. There was little use in her looking for something she had never seen and, storm or no storm, if the accounts didn't get done the farm would be sunk anyway.

Gruff led Mat to the toolshed and they peered into the cool, dim interior of the small stone building. A line of square windows marched across the back wall, but they were grimy with cobwebs and there was very little light. Gruff ran to the farmhouse for torches and he and Mat began picking through the boxes of dusty, rusty tools of generations past. Hoes and trowels, pokers and saws. In one corner stood a huge, weighty anvil, piled high with boxes of shapeless metal lumps, horseshoes, sheep bells and nails, and an entire crate of hammers, none of which was the right one. Gruff couldn't shake the niggling feeling that they were looking in the wrong place, but he couldn't think where else to try.

'What will happen if I put the sword down?' Mat asked.

Gruff looked up from the ancient mouse nest he had just found under a pile of flowerpots. 'I don't know.'

'It's hurting my arm. Shall I try?'

Gruff watched as she carefully placed the hilt down on the shed floor and released her grip.

The hilt melted instantly away into a puddle of water. Mat gasped. 'Oh no! What if I can't get it back?'

'I … I don't know.'

'I'll be back,' Mat said, already on her way out of the toolshed. Gruff watched her run across the farmyard, heading for the nearest bit of sea, and then carried on his search. He opened boxes and poked down the back of shelves. He picked gingerly through the contents of rotting canvas bags. He glanced occasionally at the puddle of dirty water in the middle of the floor. He hoped Mat could recall the sword.

Gruff couldn't move the anvil, even with all the boxes off it, but he climbed on top and shone his torch down behind. There was something there, a leather pouch hanging from a nail. He unhooked the bag and pulled open the drawstring, shining his torch into it.

Inside was the hammer.

Gruff made a sort of excited hiccup. But when he pulled the hammer out, his relief turned to disappointment. This hammer was too small, too light. He tapped it with his fingernail and realised it was made of wood, stained grey to resemble metal or stone. It was only the length of his hand, a toy. But in all other respects it was exactly like the hammer he had seen hanging at the blacksmith's belt. It had the same blocky head and thick handle, carved with plants and animals – a snake-bodied, dog-headed beast, a bird, a bear. Everything was perfect in miniature. Gruff ran his finger carefully over the beautiful carving, knowing that if he wasn't so disappointed he would be impressed by the workmanship.

He carried the hammer into the daylight and perched on an upside-down bucket to inspect it more closely. The person who'd made this had seen the real thing. The proof was there, in every painstakingly carved line.

Gruff had hung the bag over his arm by its drawstring; now he turned it inside out, to check he hadn't missed anything. A scrap of folded paper fluttered to the ground. He pounced on it as the wind tried to whip it away across the yard. It looked old – slightly grey and very thin. Very carefully, he unfolded it. It was covered in Welsh, written in pencil in a looping but untidy hand, as though the writer had once been taught a beautiful cursive but had never really used it. The spelling was old-fashioned, and Gruff had to read it slowly to get every word.

The hammer of the blacksmith.
Last seen in 1549 by Gareth ap Ifan, then a child.
The jetty was swept away the next day and many lives were lost. Gareth carved the hammer, and when he was a master blacksmith himself he gave it to his apprentice to preserve, along with a legend that the hammer will be needed to finish a sword.
I do not know whether the hammer in the legend is this one, or whether this wooden toy is just a replica.
Perhaps the whole thing is simply a story.
I have no apprentice to pass the hammer on to. I am writing what I know about the hammer here,

and I will put it somewhere safe in the hopes that a
blacksmith comes after me to continue the tradition.
Whatever the truth of the story, the wooden hammer
is a beautiful thing.
The inscription was added by fisherman Tomos ap
Rhys sometime in the 1760s. I don't know why.
Aled ap Owain, 3 June 1886

Gruff read the note three times. It gave him the same strange feeling he sometimes got from listening to Nain and Taid and Iolo's island stories – the feeling that he was simply a pinprick of life, a moment in time, on this tiny rock in the immeasurable ocean. Such a feeling might have made him feel lonely and insignificant, but it did not. It was more like a warm, strong embrace of time and memory, aligning his heartbeat with that of the island.

Gareth ap Ifan had seen the ghostly blacksmith, over four hundred and fifty years ago. She had given him the same warning, the same instruction, that she had given Gruff. *Finish the sword*. Gareth had carved the hammer, perhaps to help him remember. To help him look.

He can't have finished the sword though. Because over four hundred and fifty years on, the blacksmith had appeared to Gruff.

Why now?

Finish it, or he'll kill us all.

Had the danger got worse?

The jetty was swept away the next day and many lives were lost.

Would the next storm destroy the whole island?

Gruff shivered and picked the hammer up again, turning it over in his hands and marvelling at its age. What had Uncle Aled meant by someone adding an inscription in the 1760s? Did he mean the animals? But surely they were part of the original carving.

Then Gruff found it. An inscription in careful, neat block capitals on the underside of the hammer's head, the letters small but clear.

HIRAETH.

Hiraeth. The feeling of belonging and yearning and love for a place. He'd seen that somewhere, really recently...

The Weeping Stone! Gruff shot to his feet and the wind grabbed the abandoned paper and raced with it across the yard. Gruff ran after it, excitement hammering in time with his heart. Everything led back to the Weeping Stone – to the seventh Sleeper. He checked his pocket for the rock from the geology cabinet as he ran. When he caught the paper, he grabbed it with salt-wet fingers.

He folded the paper and replaced it in the bag with the replica hammer. He hung them behind the anvil and closed the shed door. He returned the torches to the house.

He pulled the small rock out of his pocket and the sea swelled in his fist.

'Gruff!' Mat came running into the yard. 'I can get it back! I tested, loads of times. It doesn't matter where I put it down, it's always back in the sea!'

'That's great,' Gruff said, distracted.

Mat looked down at his hand and frowned. 'You're dripping.'

Gruff opened his fist and showed her the stone on his palm. 'I think I know where the hammer is.'

'Matylda! Babcia Marysia's on the phone – come now or you'll miss her!' Zosia called, appearing round the corner from Blacksmith's Cottage.

Mat shot an anguished look from her mother to Gruff and back again. She itched at her neck. Gruff saw that there was a red, raw mark there. 'Tell me about it after,' she said, and he could hear what the words cost her. She went to her mum, and Gruff began to run.

He raced across the tussocky bumps of Evan's cow field and scrambled up the hill, a completely different journey in the afternoon sun from the early morning moon. Urgency pulsed through him, and excitement, and fear that he was wrong. The wind seemed first to run with him then turn and hinder him, playing with him as though he were a storm-blown leaf.

Gruff crested the summit of the hill. The Weeping Stone – the seventh Sleeper – was dry and empty. No blacksmith, no picnickers. Gruff clambered up it and traced his finger over the letters he had found the day before.

HIRAETH

The shape of the letters matched those of the inscription on the replica hammer. They must both be the work of Tomos ap Rhys, fisherman on the island in the 1760s. Was it a clue to the whereabouts of the real hammer?

Hiraeth. A yearning, a belonging.

The Weeping Stone wanted to return to the sea, and the small rock wanted to return to the Weeping Stone. Gruff felt sure of this, although leaving it perched on top of the Weeping Stone last night had not worked, as it had turned up in his room again. What if the stone needed to be returned to the exact crack it had originally been chipped from?

Gruff slid back down to the ground and eyed the Weeping Stone. It was big, and it was pitted and jagged as all the Sleepers were. He held the small stone out towards the rock. 'Go on, then,' he said. 'You can move, so show me where you want to be.'

The stone remained innocently still in his palm.

Gruff moved slowly round the Weeping Stone, waving his hand up and down near it as though he was metal detecting. With each fruitless step, his heart sank. Was he really going to have to find one crack amongst so many? He wouldn't finish checking over the whole stone before his birthday next year, let alone before the storm. He came full circle to where he had started, and climbed back up the stone so he could reach the higher bits. He'd really hoped this would work.

The stone in his palm twitched.

Gruff gasped and looked down at it, but it was still again. He ran his fingers over the surface of the Weeping Stone where his hand had stopped, and found a crevice. A crevice that seemed to be the right size, the right shape.

Taking a deep breath and preparing himself for disappointment, Gruff leant over the edge of the Weeping Stone and carefully pushed the small, brine-wet rock into the hole.

It slotted in like the final satisfying piece of a jigsaw puzzle. In an instant, the crack around it fused as though it had never been there. Crouched on top of the Weeping Stone, Gruff waited on tenterhooks, not sure what to do next.

A tremendous, ear-pulsing CRACK rent the air. Gruff flinched and lost his balance. As he began to fall he saw the blacksmith's hammer, resting snugly in the surface of the Weeping Stone as though it had always been there. He flung out his arm and scrabbled at it as he slipped, stubbing his fingers and just managing to get a grip on the handle.

He was on the ground, the breath knocked out of him. He lay on his back and gasped quick, noisy gulps of air, triumph pounding through his veins and the blacksmith's hammer clutched tightly in his hand.

Chapter 20

'Blacksmith!' Gruff gasped, as soon as he had enough breath to speak. He pushed himself to his feet, the hammer heavy in his hand. 'Blacksmith!'

No reply. The Weeping Stone was just a stone and Gruff was alone on the hilltop with an ancient hammer and the wind for company.

Gareth ap Ifan had missed some of the detail of the handle's carving in his wooden replica. Here, the bear reared on its back legs and raised its paws to birds in the vine-like tree above. A mouse and a squirrel chased one another through the vegetation. The dog-headed beast's body became the tree itself, all the animals linked together in an interconnected knot. The carving was still and solid, not like the moving decoration on the sword.

The hammer was formed from a single piece of stone. It had left behind a hammer-shaped hole in the Weeping Stone, a fresh, sharp-edged wound with no weathering or lichen. The blacksmith had chipped her hammer from the living rock and used it to give form to water. After the accident, it must have been returned to its mother-stone. Hidden. Safe. Waiting.

The hammer felt good in his hand: heavy and real. This wasn't going to suddenly burst into water droplets. Gruff swung it experimentally. He thought about hitting the Weeping Stone but decided against it. Who knew what would happen if he did that.

Triumph rose in him again and he punched his hand to the air, hammer held high. 'I did it!' he shouted into the face of the wind. He laughed. 'I did it!'

Finish the sword.

Finish it, or he'll kill us all.

Gruff sighed. 'Well, anyway. I did a bit of it.'

Raindrops began to patter softly around him.

'We can do this,' Gruff whispered. He slid down the hill, the rain quickly turning the path to mud, and set off across Evan's field.

As he climbed the gate back into the farm, his phone buzzed in his pocket. He took it out and checked it before he remembered he was expecting a text. He'd been so intent on trying to help the island, he'd not been thinking about the fact he might have to leave it. But when he saw who the text was from, the hammer was forgotten.

Mam.

Gruff stopped in his tracks and opened the text,

his heart thumping painfully and rain running down his neck and dripping off his chin.

Sweetheart, what's brought this on? Of course you can, if that's what you want. I could fix up the study, turn it into a bedroom. I do most of my work at the kitchen table anyway. I'll ring later. Love you xxxx

Raindrops splattered the screen and blurred the words. Gruff looked at his home, the low grey farmhouse with its steep roof and crooked chimney, as though it was a photograph of somewhere he had known long ago. Nostalgic. No longer his.

'Gruff!' Dad appeared at the back door, waving an arm to get his attention. 'Where's your coat? You'll catch your death!'

Gruff shoved his phone back into his pocket and ran the last hundred yards to the house, going round it to the front door so he could abandon his muddy trainers there and avoid a lecture from Nain. He stood in the hall in soggy socks, realising how wet and cold he was. Dad was whistling through his teeth in the kitchen and Nain had moved her accounting inside; he could see her stationed in the living room in her armchair, deeply focused on her spreadsheets. He had an unsettling feeling that he was not really there – that he could see and hear his family but they could not see him. That he was already gone, and Dad, whistling in the kitchen, was making dinner for just two.

Gruff dug his fingernails into his palm. *I'll visit in the holidays*, he promised himself. *It's not like I can't ever come back.* The text seemed to make his pocket horribly heavy. He wished Mam hadn't said yes. He wished he'd never asked her.

'Gruff!' Dad stuck his head out of the kitchen. 'You're sopping! Get changed, now. I don't want to be calling the air ambulance out for a case of self-inflicted pneumonia.' His eyes flicked down to Gruff's hand. 'What's that?'

Gruff looked down at the hammer, feeling slightly surprised that it was still there. 'Um … a hammer.'

'I can see that.' Dad emerged from the kitchen, dusting floury hands on his trousers. Gruff held the hammer up for him to see.

'What beautiful markings,' Dad said. He put his hand out and Gruff gave the hammer to him without thinking, and then felt a sudden spike of panic that it might disappear or something – but it did not. Dad turned it over in his hands, admiring it.

'It's made of stone. How strange!' Dad said. 'Where did you find it? In the shed?'

'Owain!' Nain called from the living room. 'I thought the Woolly Warmers shop was asking for more stock?'

Dad's face fell, worry settling into the tight line of his mouth. He handed the hammer back to Gruff and went to join Nain in the living room. 'They didn't have a good year themselves,' he said quietly as he closed the door. 'They don't want any new stock from us.' The latch clicked shut and Gruff was alone.

The text still sat heavy in his pocket, but balancing it against Dad's worry made it seem somehow lighter. This. *This* was why he should be glad Mam had said yes.

He had been going to tell Dad about the hammer, but now he didn't want to add to the worry etched into his face. Also, Dad would probably just try and stop Gruff from being involved, in case he got hurt. Dad could be like that sometimes. Barrelled down by a sheep, no problem, but stand in the rain without a coat for five minutes and he became all parent-y.

He *would* tell Dad. Just not yet.

Gruff climbed the stairs, leaving damp footprints on the threadbare carpet, and changed into dry clothes. His wet ones were muddy but that would brush off when they were dry. He took them downstairs and hung them on the clothes horse in the living room. The worried conversation about Woolly

161

Warmers had finished: Dad was back in the kitchen whistling as though nothing had happened and Nain had disappeared.

Gruff sat on the rug, next to a sleeping Hywel. He put the hammer at his feet and traced the lines of the beautifully carved handle with his finger. How long would it be before he wouldn't be here to sit in his favourite spot on the rug anymore?

Nain gasped as she came into the room. 'You found it?'

Gruff grinned despite himself. 'Yup.'

'Tell me everything!'

As Gruff helped Nain file the papers and put the folding table away in the corner of the room he explained what had happened since he and Mat had left Nain in the garden. Nain inspected the hammer with her glasses perched on the end of her nose. 'Incredible,' she whispered. She looked up at Gruff. 'So what next?'

Gruff took a shaky breath and smiled. 'Now I guess we have to finish the sword.'

Finish it, or he'll kill us all.

'Before the storm,' Gruff added, reaching out to take the hammer back. He weighed it in his hand, this ancient, magical object hidden in stone for longer than memory. 'Finish the sword before the storm.'

Beside him, Hywel whined in his sleep.

Chapter 21

'So what do we need to do?' Mat asked, sword in hand. She knelt on the edge of the jetty near the lifeboat slip, Gruff beside her. The morning wind was half-heartedly throwing raindrops at them after a wet night. They had escaped together to see if they could finish what the blacksmith had started. Excitement fluttered like a trapped bird in Gruff's chest.

'She ducked the sword in and out of the sea seven times,' Gruff said, 'and then she held it underwater and hit it with the hammer seven times.'

Mat stroked the carved handle of the hammer, lying on the wooden boards between them.

'I think you should do it,' Gruff said. 'The blacksmith did it all herself, and you're the only one who can touch the sword.'

Mat wrapped her fingers round the hammer's handle and made a small noise of surprise. Gruff saw that the tendons in her wrist were taut with the effort of trying to lift the hammer, but it did not budge.

'That's strange,' Gruff said. 'Dad and Nain could pick it up.'

Mat let go of the sword hilt and it scattered as water down into the sea. She wrapped both hands round the handle of the hammer and yanked hard. The hammer came up without any problem at all and she fell over backwards, laughing. 'Oops!' Hammer in hand, she bent down and fished for the sword again.

'Got it,' she said, but then the hammer fell out of her grasp and hit the jetty with a dull thunk. 'Oh,' she said. 'It got heavy.'

Gruff frowned and picked the hammer up, turning it over in his hand. 'So you can't hold the hammer if you're holding the sword?'

'Yeah, I think so.'

A little surge of pleasure flared in Gruff's fingertips. Maybe he was needed after all. 'Perhaps we can do it together,' he said.

Mat grinned, nodding first towards the hammer, and then to the fluid hilt in her hand. 'You're the land and I'm the water.' Her smile faltered.

'You okay?' Gruff asked.

Mat shrugged. 'Yeah, fine.' She looked down at the hilt in her wet hand. 'I just … water doesn't really belong anywhere, does it?'

'Oh … I don't know.'

Gruff wasn't sure what she meant, or why it would make her look so forlorn. He couldn't see anything upsetting about being the only person able to hold a magical sword. He hefted the hammer in his grip. 'Do you want to try, then?'

'Yeah.' Mat bent down to the slapping wavelets and plunged the sword's invisible blade and decorated hilt into the cold water. 'One.' She drew it out and plunged it back in. 'Two. Three. Four. Five. Six. Seven.'

After the seventh plunge Mat turned to look at Gruff expectantly. Gruff shuffled closer, gripping the hammer. He aimed for where he thought the length of the sword had got to and brought the hammer down as hard as he could against the resistance of the water.

There was no connection, no ringing note. The hammer met nothing but sea, and the determination of Gruff's swing almost carried him straight over the edge of the jetty. He pulled himself up with difficulty and tried another swing, this time very close to the hilt, where he knew there should be sword blade to connect with.

Nothing.

Gruff sat back, dripping seawater and raindrops.

'It didn't work.' The disappointment was all the worse because he'd been so excited since he'd pulled the hammer from the Weeping Stone the day before. He'd even pushed aside thoughts of Mam and leaving – even ignored the fact that Mam had said she would ring, and had not – because the thought of finishing the sword had kept him going through the night, through the seven o'clock hen feeding and egg collecting, through helping out in the wool barn, through the walk to the jetty, which they had chosen as being the safest place to get out above deep water without fear of falling in.

'The jetty,' Gruff said.

Mat was slumped, rubbing her wet hand to get some feeling back into it. 'That's where we are,' she said unnecessarily.

'What if that's what's wrong?' he asked, clutching for straws of hope. 'What if the place is important?'

Mat stopped rubbing her fingers. 'The seventh Sleeper?'

'But it's not there anymore,' Gruff said, half to himself. He eyed Rosie Small's little rowing boat bobbing against the jetty behind them and felt a bit queasy. 'We'd never get a boat to stay in the right place – the current's too strong and there's no way to anchor one.'

'We could swim,' Mat said quietly.

Fear trickled down Gruff's spine. 'But you *can't* swim,' he said. 'I mean, I know you did the other night, but you forgot who you were … it was scary. And I can't swim in that current either.'

'I remembered I'm me after, though.' Mat turned

to him, her brown eyes steady and serious. 'If I did it then, I can do it again.'

Gruff shook his head, slowly. 'But, Mat –'

'My choice,' Mat interrupted. 'I'm going in. You don't have to come.'

'I do if you can't hold the hammer.' Gruff huffed crossly. 'You weren't there the other night, Mat.'

'Yes, I was!'

'But you don't remember!' Gruff thought of the girl on the beach, full of the power of the sea. The girl who had turned from him to walk back into the waves. 'What if you don't remember again?'

'My choice,' Mat said. She stood up, scratching at the irritated skin on her neck. 'Coming?'

Gruff watched her walk away from him up the jetty. Going out to the Sleepers again was a terrible idea. They were lucky to have survived once. And what if Mat forgot who she was completely? What if she swam away and didn't come back?

But what would happen if they failed to finish the sword? What might the storm bring? What might Dylan do?

'Wait!' Gruff called, and he ran to catch up with her. 'We'll need wetsuits.'

*

Gruff dug the wetsuits out from the bottom of his jumper drawer. Luckily there were two. He'd got a new one for his birthday because the old one was getting a bit tight. He squeezed into his old one and let Mat have the brand-new one. It was her who needed maximum movability. If all went well, he shouldn't have to do much swimming at all.

'We need to tell someone where we're going,' Gruff said, when Mat came out of the bathroom wearing his new wetsuit, turning her plaits into a ponytail to keep her hair out of the way.

'What'll we say?' she asked. 'We're just going in the sea, even though I can't swim and Gruff nearly drowned the other night, no biggie.'

Gruff snorted. It shouldn't have been funny, but her sarcasm was on point. Mat grinned. 'You know they'll just tell us not to.'

He sucked air through his teeth and imagined himself explaining to Nain and Dad what they were planning. At last he settled on sticking his head over the wool barn door and calling, 'We're just going down to the beach, Dad.'

'*Iawn*,' Dad said, without looking up from the carding machine. Okay. 'You're not planning to go in the water, are you?'

Gruff's heart dropped, but he was saved from

168

either telling the truth and being banned or having to lie by Tim at the loom saying, 'Did you hear the total raised at the festival for the lifeboat?'

'No,' Dad said. 'Did they get enough for the renovations on the slipway?'

Gruff left them to it, feeling guilty and relieved.

'All right,' he said, meeting Mat in the middle of the yard. 'Let's go.'

As they came to the head of the beach, the pulsing pull of the Sleepers drew Gruff's eyes. To his horror, he saw little Prem half-way up the first of them, scrabbling for hand and foot-holds, scaling the mountain-like stone as though his life depended on it.

Before Gruff could start to run, he saw Prem's mother, Deepa, splashing through the ankle-deep water to her son, her basket of seaweed swinging on her arm. She reached Prem just as he was nearing the top of the Sleeper and plucked him off it. He came away like an angry starfish, waving his arms and legs and shrieking. Deepa retreated with him to the other end of the beach, Prem in floods of noisy tears.

Gruff shivered. Prem, like any island child, knew that you never, ever climbed on the Sleepers. At least he was too young to be let out of the house on his own. But what if there was a next time and he slipped away when his mum and dad weren't looking? What if he climbed out on the Sleepers when no one was around to save him from himself?

First Rosie, then Mat, now Prem. The stones were calling and nobody was safe.

Deepa was heading back towards the fishermen's cottages, Prem held firmly by the hand. He was still wailing and looking back at the tempting line of the Sleepers.

'We should wait for her to go inside,' Mat said. 'She might try and stop us.'

'She *would* try and stop us,' Gruff agreed. 'And she'd be right.' They watched until Deepa and Prem had disappeared inside their house, where Deepa would be turning the seaweed into her legendary laverbread and Prem would hopefully forget about the Sleepers for a while.

Gruff and Mat kicked their shoes off and put their towels under Gruff's raincoat to keep them dry, and then ran down the sand and straight into the sea before either of them could change their minds. Gruff clutched the hammer tightly in one hand, and Mat reached out for his other one. He steeled himself before wrapping his fingers round hers as the water reached their stomachs and the waves buffeted them, trying to knock them off their feet. The barrage of water from

Mat's touch pounded against Gruff's lungs. He forced himself to breathe in and out as normal, not letting the sensation trick him into thinking there really was water inside him.

Mat turned to him, grinning wildly. 'This feels so … so *right*, doesn't it?' Waves leapt in her eyes and Gruff's heart lurched.

'Not for me,' he said, forcing the words out. 'It feels all wrong. Do you know what your name is?'

Mat laughed. 'Mat!' She flipped off her feet and onto her back, and with the smallest flick of her spine she was moving through the water. Gruff found himself dragged after her, kicking desperately, the hammer weighing him down. He felt like a newborn lamb, all arms and legs and no control over any of them.

Mat stopped and Gruff looked up to see the sixth Sleeper towering high above them. He couldn't tread water with the hammer in one hand and his other in Mat's, and he only got a glimpse of the stone before the water closed over his head. He felt the tug of the current against his body and swallowed the panic rising in him, as Mat readjusted her grip, wrapping one arm tightly around his chest and yanking him up to the surface. He broke through and found that they hadn't moved a centimetre. She paddled her feet slowly in the water, keeping them both steady.

Gruff's teeth were chattering but Mat's cheeks were flushed with excitement. She drew her left hand out of the water, the hilt shining in her grip. 'Here we go,' she grinned. She plunged it into the water and pulled it out, and plunged it in again. And again, and again. 'Ready?' she asked as she ducked the sword under for the seventh time.

Gruff brought his hammer hand round and drove it towards the invisible blade, just below the hilt.

The hammer passed straight through.

'No!' Gruff hissed. '*No*.'

'Gruff!' Mat shouted.

Gruff looked up from his failed hammer strike and saw a great wave drawing itself up from the swell, sweeping towards them, three times the height of the waves around it. Within the wave he saw the face of a man, contorted in a silent scream of pain and fury.

Chapter 22

The sea had a face and it was looking at him. The sea had arms and they ended in webbed fingers, outstretched to envelope him in a deadly embrace.

Gruff had time for one true thought, and that was, *Breathe*.

So he did. He took a single, deep, precious breath of salty air before the wave arrived, carrying cold, scrabbling hands that tried to tear the hammer from his grasp even as the water pushed Gruff and Mat back and slammed them painfully against the sixth Sleeper.

Mat still had him gripped in one arm. That was all that stopped Gruff from flailing panic, all that stopped him from dropping the hammer to try and escape those fingers and find the surface again. He brought his feet up and pushed them against the chest of his attacker, invisible in the broiling, stinging water. Mat shifted her grip round Gruff's middle and pulled him away from Dylan, away from the rock, away from the heaving sea.

They did not break the surface immediately. Gruff

squeezed his eyes shut against the rush of cold water and sensed the strength in Mat's body as she flicked and twisted through the current. He clung onto the hammer and imagined Dylan chasing them through the waves, slick as a seal, angry and strong. But they would reach land soon, and hopefully he couldn't follow them there.

Surely they would reach land soon?

Gruff could hold his breath for forty-six seconds, he'd timed himself once. The tight uncertainty in his lungs now told him he had only about ten seconds left. He cracked his eyes open and saw flickering, brighter water above him, the surface maybe three feet away. He shifted in Mat's grip and tried to reach for the air. Mat's arm was a clamp round his middle, far stronger than he had expected. He tapped her on the back, but she made no sign she was aware of him.

'Mat!' he gargled through the water, wasting precious air. He tugged at her encircling arm. 'Mat!'

To his eternal relief, she brought him up to the surface.

Gruff breathed deeply and made a failed attempt to wipe the water from his eyes. The air was cold and the waves choppy. He blinked and looked around, first seeing Mat's head bobbing beside him, her eyes leaping wild – and then seeing the island.

It was a frighteningly long way away. He could

see the whole of the east coast. He could see the two headlands and the beach between. He could see the small grey cluster of farm buildings to the left, and round the other side he could see the gash in the cliff that sheltered the lifeboat slipway.

Panic rose up his throat. 'Why are we here? Why didn't you take us to shore?'

Mat laughed and began to pull him down into the water again.

'No!' The word came out as a half-scream and Gruff wrenched himself out of her grip. 'Mat! Are you there? Come back!' The weight of the hammer dragged at him and he trod water desperately with his free hand. 'Come back!'

The smile left Mat's face. 'Gruff.'

Gruff held his chin up out of the slapping water. 'Yes. I'm Gruff. You're Mat.' He shivered violently, the cold heavy in his limbs. 'Please remember!'

Mat's face drew tight with fear. 'Of course I'm Mat. Where are we?'

Relief made Gruff grin. 'You swam us here.'

Mat shook her head. The sea had gone from her eyes. 'No, I didn't. I didn't.'

'You did. Dylan was there. You rescued us and swam us out to sea.' A wave washed into Gruff's mouth and he coughed and pushed his chin higher.

Mat turned to look for the island. She gasped.

'Yup,' Gruff said grimly.

'I didn't!' Shrill panic rose in Mat's voice.

Gruff struggled over and put a hand on her arm. 'Let's just swim back.'

She looked at him in terror. 'I don't know how.'

'You swam out here.'

'It wasn't me!'

'Come on, Mat. You can do this.' Gruff forced a smile. Clutching the hammer to his chest, he turned onto his back. With his free hand holding tight to Mat's elbow, he began to kick out for the island through the icy water. 'Turn on your back … yeah, like that. And kick your legs. Okay, I'm going to let go of you, and you just need to bring your arms up and round your head, one after the other. Like a windmill. Okay?'

'Okay,' Mat muttered, staring straight up at the sky and not looking at him. 'Okay.'

She swam hesitantly and with much splashing. Every few seconds her legs failed her and she sank underwater, coming back up spluttering and increasingly panicked. Gruff tried to keep her calm, talking all he could, telling her that she was doing brilliantly. It was only her mounting fear that kept his own at bay.

After two minutes, Gruff knew they weren't going

to make it. Even with the heavy hammer, he was doing better than Mat. He could drop it, abandon it to the sea, and try to support Mat all the way back to the island, but he knew he wasn't strong enough for the journey. And at any moment they could be attacked by Dylan, returning in a wave to swamp them. That threat made his skin crawl worse than any thought of sharp-toothed seals, stinging jellyfish or massive whales below.

There was only one thing he could think of.

He turned his head to Mat, struggling beside him, and smiled brightly. 'Mat. Remember when you swam us out here? And when you saved my life the other night?'

'No.'

'But it was *you*, wasn't it?' Gruff insisted. 'You're amazing. You swim like an eel. This is your place, isn't it? The sea's calling to you. It's your home.' He hated himself for encouraging Mat to not be herself. But they were going to sink, out here in the Irish Sea, and no one would even know what had happened. 'You belong in the water.'

Mat turned to him. 'Really?' she asked, her voice suddenly strong. Waves leapt in her eyes.

Gruff forced himself to keep eye contact. She had to believe this, right now. 'Yes.'

Mat grinned, her fear forgotten. She wrapped her arm tightly across Gruff's back, supporting him, and began to move swiftly and effortlessly through the slapping waves. Gruff breathed in short, quick bursts to try and avoid getting a nose full of salt water. He hoped Mat wouldn't suddenly take it into her head to dive or head away from the island again.

In less than a minute, the water calmed. Gruff twisted round and saw they were in the cove with the lifeboat slipway and the wooden jetty he and Mat had been on just an hour before. Mat swam them alongside the jetty and Gruff gripped the rough planks, swinging the hammer up and hoisting himself after it. Dry land. Relief filled his limbs with jelly.

Gruff reached his hand out to Mat, but she just smiled and shook her head. She flipped over and disappeared beneath the surface.

'Come back!' Gruff yelled. He saw her dark form slip through the water to the head of the cove and away. He stared after her, his mind numb. This was his fault. He'd persuaded her to go into her swimming dream-state.

What if she never came back?

The wind whipped the water from his cheeks, leaving them caked with salt. He strained his eyes across the waves. He should raise the alarm. They should send out a search party.

He was just about to turn and run for help when he saw something in the mouth of the cove. Mat surfaced, bobbing there like a seal. Gruff's heart leapt. 'Mat!'

She grinned and waved to him. 'Come in, it's fun!'

Relief was replaced by dread. 'No,' he said. He shuffled back from the edge. 'I'm not coming in. You have to come out.'

'Boring. I'm coming to get you!' Mat ducked under and reappeared right next to the jetty, moving as fast as a flying swallow. She reached out one wetsuited arm and grabbed for his leg.

Gruff leapt backwards out of reach. 'Stop it!'

'Come on!'

It took all his restraint not to run away and leave her there. He thought quickly. 'How about you come out, and we jump off the end of the jetty together? That'd be fun, right?'

Mat grinned. 'Yes!' She pulled herself up and out of the water. He backed away as she stumbled towards him. Her breathing sounded forced and strange.

'Hi, Mat,' Gruff said. He took another step backwards. He hadn't thought this through. He'd just wanted her out of the water, but he could see that her eyes were still not her own. Within them was the swell of a pre-thunderstorm sea, water thick and heavy with danger.

Not knowing what else to do, Gruff pulled words out as fast as he could. He had to get Mat to remember herself. 'You're Matylda Kowalska and your mum is called Zosia and your step-dad is called John, and you've just moved here from Manchester and you're going to be an oceanologist. And you told me how angelsharks are found round the Welsh coast and they're protected because they're critically endangered, and you told me that seal milk is fifty percent fat and that's why baby seals grow so quickly. And you told me that plankton and other tiny things are just as important to protect as the big animals because of the ecosystem, and you know loads about the sea but really you're a human and you live on land and you're not Dylan and you swam out there –' he waved his hand to the open water – 'and woke up and you were scared because you didn't remember doing it. You were scared because *that wasn't you.*'

She stopped and Gruff stayed very still. He was ready to run away if he needed to, ready to call for help if she jumped back in. 'Mat?'

Mat nodded slowly. Her knees buckled and she came down hard on the planks of the jetty, not bothering to stop her fall. Gruff jumped forward and caught her before her head hit the ground. She put her hands out and pushed against the rough planks, struggling upwards. 'I'm okay,' she whispered.

'You're back.'

'I think so.' Mat sat cross-legged. Gruff sat opposite her. They stared at one another in silence.

Mat coughed. 'What happened?'

'You went swimming.'

'I can't breathe properly.' She reached up to her sodden ponytail and pulled the bobble out. Gruff gasped. She frowned at him. 'What?'

He shuffled forward and put his hand out. 'Mat...' He lifted her hair out of the way. His voice sounded strange in his own ears. 'Mat, you've got gills.'

Chapter 23

Mat sat in the kitchen of the farmhouse and fingered the raw, red flaps of skin on both sides of her neck. Gruff winced. 'Does it hurt?'

She shook her head. 'Not exactly. It just feels weird.' She snorted with uncertain laughter. 'I'm turning into a fish!'

He shrugged one shoulder, not wanting to upset her. She did appear to be turning into a fish.

Mat ran her hands up her arms. 'You said Dylan had scales?'

'Yeah.' Gruff tried to imagine Mat looking like Dylan had. Would she stop being able to come on land? Would she forget herself forever? It was hard to believe any of it, sitting quietly at the pitted wooden table of the farmhouse kitchen, with the saucepans hanging on the wall and the gingham lampshade and the peeling paint above the window. It would be impossible to believe, if Mat wasn't sitting opposite him poking at her gills with an expression of curiosity and horror. 'Are you going to tell your mum and John?'

She fidgeted with the pepper pot. 'I want to. I mean, I wanted to tell them about the sword and stuff, but what if they don't believe me? What if they think I'm lying, and they stop trusting me or –'

'Mat,' Gruff said firmly. 'You have gills. They've got to believe you.'

'Oh yeah.' She grinned sheepishly. 'Do you think I'll go back to normal when we finish the sword?'

'I don't know.' Secretly, he didn't think what was happening to Mat was anything to do with the sword. She'd told him she used to walk too far into the sea when she was a small child, and that was long before she came to the island. Perhaps whatever was happening to her now had always been waiting to come out.

'I mean, I don't hate it,' Mat said quietly. 'I know it's weird and everything, but when I remember what it feels like to be part of the water, it's like … it's like coming home. What did you say the word was? I feel *hiraeth* for the sea. You know you asked me if I felt like the sea was inside me, the other day? I didn't know what you meant, then, but I can feel it now. I think it's always been there, but I didn't notice it. Like the way you don't notice your heartbeat because it's just normal. The sea's inside me. It's always been inside me.'

Dad's mobile, abandoned on the kitchen sideboard, rang. Gruff got up and checked the display. *Eleri*. His heart plummeted. Not now. He didn't want this conversation now. And why hadn't she rung him? He went to check his own phone and realised he'd left it in his room.

The front door latch clicked up. Dad's voice came through from the hallway: 'Oh, the phone's ringing.'

Looking panicked, Mat shook her hair out over her neck and stood up. Gruff, seeing no way out, answered the phone.

'Hi, Mam,' he said, just as Dad walked into the kitchen with Nain, Tim and Elen behind him.

Dad mouthed, 'Who is it?'

'Mam,' Gruff mouthed back. Dad's eyebrows went up in surprise, but he didn't offer to take the phone. He went to the bread bin and pulled out a loaf.

'Hello, *cariad*,' Mam said. 'I rang you but you didn't pick up. Are you okay? What brought on that text?'

'Um,' Gruff said. His mind spun away from him and he couldn't seem to find words to answer. Dad was cutting the bread as Tim ladled soup into bowls and Elen filled the kettle. Mat hovered in the doorway, looking at Gruff with pleading eyes. She hadn't been prepared for an influx of people either.

'Sweetheart?' Mam said.

Gruff headed for the door. 'Sorry, Mam. Everyone just came in to make lunch.'

Mat escaped into the hall ahead of him. 'I'm going home,' she whispered. He nodded and she disappeared outside, coughing.

Gruff took the stairs two at a time and lay on his bed. He stared up at the cobweb-covered ceiling, watching Gary the spider and the Garyettes lurking quiet and patient in their sticky homes.

'Gruff? Are you still there?'

'Yes.' *Not for much longer*, he thought. 'I … I just … the farm is in trouble, and if I wasn't here, maybe it'd help.'

'Oh, Gruff!' Mam sounded shocked and angry. 'Did Dad say that?'

'No!' Gruff shook his head violently even though she couldn't see him. 'No, Dad doesn't even know I sent the text.'

'This is a big decision, *cariad*. You've got to talk to your dad about it.'

'Well, I can't tell him and you at the same time, so I had to start somewhere.' The words came out more bitterly than he'd meant them to.

Mam sighed. 'If it's really what you want, you know you're always welcome here. It's a small flat, but I'm fairly settled right now. I'm still doing a bit of travelling though. We might have to find you a friend to stay with sometimes.'

A friend. In a place he hardly knew.

'Gruff?' Mam sighed again. 'It would be a whole new start, sweetheart. New school, new friends, new way of life. No farm. You're a farming lad. Wouldn't you miss it?'

He couldn't answer. Of course he'd miss it. But if it would mean saving the farm; if it would mean having a farm to come back to and visit; if it would mean that Dad and Nain and Ffion and James and Tim and Elen and Mrs Moruzzi and all the others who looked after the sheep and spun the wool and knitted it and felted it, could carry on…

'*Cariad*, I rang now because I knew your dad would be on lunch. I'd like to talk to him, too. Do you want to tell him about the text you sent me before I do?'

'He hasn't been telling me anything about the farm,' Gruff muttered. 'He can have a surprise for once.' But the words left a nasty taste on his tongue.

'I need to talk to him now,' Mam said. 'I'll be too busy the rest of today and tomorrow.'

Gruff pushed himself off his bed, feeling heavy and tired.

'I need to know one more thing before I talk to

Dad,' Mam said, in her most firm, Mam-like voice. 'Do you want to leave the island? Tell me truthfully, Gruffydd.'

'No,' Gruff said, coming down the stairs slowly and wishing they were twice as long. 'I don't want to leave.'

'Then why, Gruff? This is a big thing to have asked. To ask of your dad and your nain. To ask of yourself.'

Gruff felt very young and small. Tears pricked unhelpfully at the back of his eyes. He sat down on the final step of the stairs and rested his forehead on his hand. 'We can't lose the farm, Mam. Dad and Nain mustn't leave the island.'

'A sacrifice,' Mam said. 'How noble.' She sighed. 'My brave boy, carrying the weight of the farm on his shoulders. It's not your weight to carry, sweetheart.'

Gruff gulped and half-laughed. He thought of the hammer and the sword and the blacksmith and the storm that was on its way. If only she knew.

'Lunch, Gruff?' Elen asked, appearing out of the kitchen. Her face fell when she saw him. 'Are you okay?'

'Can you get Dad?'

Elen nodded, her eyes worried. A moment later Dad came out of the kitchen, a tomato soup moustache on his top lip. He frowned.

187

'What's happened?'

'Nothing,' Gruff said quickly. 'Nothing bad, I mean. Here.' He held the phone out and Dad took it, looking mystified.

Gruff ran back up the stairs, unwilling to see Dad's face or hear the conversation. As he got to his room, he heard the front door close and he knew Dad had gone outside to talk in private. He lay on his bed and counted the Garyettes. Five. Then he deliberated over names. Peter Parker, and Fred. And Charlotte, of course. And Shelob. And Leggy.

Gruff rolled onto his side and scrunched up tight, wrapping his arms round his head as though that would protect him from all the thoughts going on inside. The money troubles and the possibility of leaving the island, and Mat becoming something that they had no word for, and the failure to finish the sword. And hanging above it all like a great, silent wave, the threat of a storm that could wash them all away.

His door clicked open and someone knocked. Dad, then. Nain was much better at remembering to do the knocking before the barging in. Gruff peered out from under his arms and saw his sturdy, dependable Dad, mud on his jeans and a hoof trimmer sticking out of one pocket, leaning on the doorframe and looking at him with glistening eyes.

Gruff pushed himself upright. Dad sniffed, rubbed a hand across his eyes and cleared his throat. 'Do you want to leave, Gruff?'

To his frustration, Gruff felt his face crumple. He'd planned this moment. He'd planned to keep a calm face and say yes. To tell Dad it was what he wanted. To make it easier for Dad to see the back of him. 'No,' Gruff whispered.

Dad moved across the room in two steps and knelt by the bed, gathering Gruff's hands into his own. 'I don't want you to leave.'

Gruff shook his head, unable to keep his tears back. 'You mustn't lose the farm. I thought, if I wasn't here … you and Nain, you'd be able to stay. And at least I'd have a farm to come back to.'

Dad took an unsteady breath. 'I would rather lose the farm than have you even think you should leave us.' He squeezed Gruff's hands. 'I know the island is where we live, but *you* are my home, Gruff, more than the island. You and Nain are my home. Do you understand?'

Gruff nodded. He couldn't speak.

'I know why you did what you did,' Dad said. 'And I'm so sorry you felt you needed to take all that worry onto yourself. I'm so sorry. I will explain everything to you properly, I promise. Tonight. After work, we'll sit

189

down and I'll tell you everything about the farm and the trouble we're in. And you'll see that you leaving the island would change nothing. But even if it did, I wouldn't let you do it. Not unless you really wanted, in your heart of hearts, to stop living with us. Yes?'

Dad pulled him into a tight, tight hug and Gruff squeezed him back, feeling safer than he had for days.

'You're my home,' Gruff whispered. 'You and Nain. You're my home.'

Chapter 24

Gruff stared at the midnight glow of his ceiling. Dad had been as good as his word, and Gruff now knew everything there was to know about the farm's finances.

It didn't look good.

Dad had told him about the accounts, the running costs of the farm and the dent in income from losing the wool through the leaking roof last year. He had told Gruff how the gift shops were struggling themselves, and the hotel that had asked for wool runners was considering getting them from a big commercial company instead. He had told him that he didn't know what else he could do.

Gruff had planned to exchange information for information and tell Dad about everything that had happened with him and Mat – but after Dad finished, Gruff just sat and stared at the patterns in the hearthrug for a long, long silent while, until Nain forced a game of dominoes on both her son and grandson to try and save the mood.

Gruff couldn't tell Dad what had happened. Dad

was worried enough as it was. And Gruff also couldn't quite bring himself to admit to Nain that he and Mat had nearly been lost at sea (again). So he kept his own news tightly locked inside his head, where it battled for space with everything Dad had told him, and a deep suspicion of Nain's made-up dominoes rules.

He put one hand out from under the duvet and felt for the hammer on his bedside table. He wrapped his fingers round the handle and held it up in front of him so that it was a dark silhouette against the ceiling. A slice of moonlight through the curtains told him it was another bright night outside. He itched to go and see it, to climb the Sleepers and watch the sea. They called him. He thought of little Prem, climbing the first. Of Rosie dropping her bucket and heading for danger. Of Mat, constantly drawn to their lure. If the Sleepers called to them in their beds, would they go?

He pushed himself up and leapt to the window, fear gripping him. Pulling back the curtain, he saw to his relief that the Sleepers were empty – and to his amazement that they were high and dry above the sea.

'Wow.' Gruff grinned. The lowest tide he had ever seen was silently sucking the sea away into the darkness. Every one of the six Sleepers reared up from glistening sand, the sea beyond a gently lapping fringe to the world.

And there was a seventh stone, and upon it a tall, cloaked figure.

Gruff was out of the house with a jumper pulled on over his pyjamas, his wellingtons dragged onto his bare feet and the hammer in his hand before he had consciously made the decision to move. He stumble-ran in the chill air, his ankles rubbing in his wellies.

'Blacksmith!' Gruff slap-thudded down the wet sand and drew up beside the seventh Sleeper, the Weeping Stone. 'Blacksmith!'

The blacksmith did not seem to hear him. She stared out to sea. The moonlight showed the smudges of soot on her clothes and face, her calloused palms, the empty loop for the hammer at her belt. A wind that was not in Gruff's night lifted the cloak on her shoulders and ruffled her hair.

'Please!' Gruff stood on the thin stretch of sand between the stone and the quiet waves and craned his neck back to see the blacksmith, waving his hands up and down as though he was trying to hail an aeroplane. 'I need to know how to finish the sword – we've tried, me and Mat, but we can't make it work. What do we need to do? Please! Blacksmith!'

No response. The sand sucked and squelched under Gruff's wellies, the sea already on the turn and beginning to lap at his heels.

'Please!'

He put his hand out to the seventh Sleeper but instead of meeting the rock, his fingers passed straight through as though the blacksmith and her stone were ghosts. *Or maybe I'm the ghost,* Gruff thought, shivering. One pinprick of time in the millennia the blacksmith had watched pass by.

Not knowing what else to try, Gruff brought the hammer up and touched it to the seventh Sleeper. It made a connection, stone on stone. There was a dull crack, like the sound of an explosion a long way off, and the impact jarred back into Gruff's elbow and sent him stumbling into the small, hungry waves. He heard a gasp and snapped his head up. The blacksmith was gazing at him as though she had never seen him before. As though she had been sleeping and woken to find herself in a strange place. Her eyes flicked to the hammer in his hand.

'*Cwblhewch y bont!*' she said. Complete the bridge.

The bridge? Nain's old song said the Sleepers were bridging something. Did the blacksmith want him to put the Weeping Stone back on the beach?

'How?' Gruff called. 'I don't know how!'

The blacksmith touched the empty hammer loop at her belt. 'They want to be together.'

Gruff looked down at the hammer in his hand.

What did she mean? That the hammer needed to be back with her? He reached up and tried to hand it over, but the blacksmith made no move to take it – and a moment later, she and the stone were gone.

'Come back!' he shouted. 'Come back!' He kicked the soft sand where the stone had been. The sea bubbled up to fill the hole and still he was alone. How could he return the hammer to her if she didn't even try to take it?

Unless … unless that wasn't what she had meant.

The hammer was carved from the Weeping Stone itself, the lonely seventh Sleeper that had been moved so many years ago. Was the blacksmith telling him that the hammer wanted to be with the Weeping Stone? But if that was the case, how come Gruff had been able to pull the hammer free in the first place?

'Oh,' Gruff said softly, and he stepped forward into the space where the seventh Sleeper had once stood. *They* want to be together. It wasn't an instruction to give the hammer to the blacksmith, or to take it back where he had found it. It was a fact. The seven Sleepers wanted to be together, and the hammer was the key.

Gruff ran his thumb over the decorated stone of the hammer's handle. A piece of the Weeping Stone, of the seventh Sleeper itself. 'You belong here,' he said. 'This is your home.' He touched the head of the hammer down to the wet sand and an almost painful sense of excitement, intertwined with loneliness and longing, hit him so strongly he nearly let go. He took several careful breaths, hope bringing a grin to his face. Then he wrapped his other hand round the hammer's handle and walked in a wide circle, dragging the hammer through the sand and leaving a trail behind. The sea bubbled and bloomed into the track. Yearning rocked him, the emotions of someone else – some*thing* else.

He completed the outline of the place where the seventh Sleeper ought to stand and lifted the hammer from the line with difficulty, the desperate homesickness now coming over him in physical waves that made his legs tremble and his arms weak. He stood in the centre of his creation and watched the sea creep nearer.

The circle looked complete but didn't feel it. It was as though he had missed something, like forgetting to dot an i in a sentence. Like an electrical circuit without any power, ready to spark to life but unable to do so. He'd outlined the body of the stone, but not its heart.

He dropped to his knees, swinging the hammer round and down. The stone head thudded into the soft, sucking sand in the very centre of the circle.

A desperate, aching shock of need and want. Gruff stayed on his knees, the wet sand soaking into his pyjamas and the sea running into the tops of his wellies. He couldn't move; his hands seemed glued around the handle of the hammer and the hammer was too heavy to lift. His whole body shook with the emotions coursing through it.

He knew, with a wild, moonlit clarity, that the Weeping Stone was on the move.

Chapter 25

Gruff didn't know how long he knelt there, but he was suddenly aware that his wellies were completely flooded and the sea was over his knees and washing around his wrists. His hands were still clenched round the hammer, channelling the excitement of a stone that was on its way, would arrive in this very place. Would crush him if he was still there to meet it.

He had to move.

Gruff stared at the hammer, unsure what to do. It seemed to be melded to the sand of the beach, impossibly heavy in his hands. But if he left it here and it reunited with the seventh Sleeper tonight, how could he use it to finish the sword?

He stood up so that he was stooped instead of kneeling, still holding the hammer in both hands. He braced himself and pulled upwards, hard. The hammer came away as light as a feather and the surprise of it sent him staggering backwards.

Gruff ran from the circle and up the beach. He still felt the Weeping Stone's longing and hope, but the sensation was less now, manageable. He made it back to the comforting familiarity of the farmyard and paused outside the front door to pour the last of the seawater from his wellies. He wondered if he had made the right decision, taking the hammer away from the beach.

And then he heard it.

A slow, insistent scraping, dragging – the sound of something large and heavy ploughing through resistant ground. Quiet at first and then louder; never pausing, never changing pace. As relentless as the onward movement of a glacier, carving the ground it passes over. From the direction of Evan's field it came, louder and louder. Towards the farm.

Unearthly. That was the only word Gruff could think of. The sound poured into his veins as a deep, ancient fear.

He yanked his wellies back on and reached for the safety of the farmhouse, but stopped with his hand on the latch. What if the stone was following the hammer? What if it came after him, and ploughed straight into his home?

Slowly, every muscle screaming at him to turn back, Gruff skirted the farmhouse and walked towards the noise. Round the side of the sleeping Blacksmith's Cottage he went, the sound growing and grating in his bones – and there it was. The horizon of Evan's field had been altered. A great moving mountain cast a black shape against the night sky.

'Hi,' Gruff said. 'Fancy seeing you here.'

The Weeping Stone ploughed on, moving at a constant speed through earth and grass and rocky ground. Gruff watched, ready to run if he needed to, but after a few moments he saw that the stone was not moving towards him and the hammer clutched in his fist. It was passing them by, on a beeline from hill to beach.

On its way to join its siblings.

Phew, Gruff thought. But then he looked at the route the stone was taking. There were two crashes coming up.

He might be able to avoid one of them.

He put the hammer safely to one side and scrambled over the wall into Top Field, running to fumble at the twine securing the gate between it and Evan's field. The gate hadn't been opened for a long time, and the twine's knots were swollen with rain. The stone bore inexorably down on him.

'Come *on*,' Gruff whispered. He dragged at the knot, hardly even able to see it in the dark, preparing himself to leap out of the way and abandon the gate to its fate and the farm to another unexpected expense.

The knot loosened and Gruff tore the twine away

and yanked the gate up out of its rut, pulling and lifting. Through came the stone, just clearing the gatepost, the noise deafening, the ground shuddering, the gate's rusted bars flaking under the onslaught of movement and sound.

On it went, away from him, the shocking intensity of its nearness holding Gruff frozen. He stared at the deep, churned rut the stone had left behind. Smaller rocks poked up, and roots, and metal edges that suggested farm tools long lost. Confused earthworms, panicked beetles.

Gruff lifted the gate back into position and re-tied the twine. The Weeping Stone trailed away over Top Field, heading straight for the beach and the Sleepers. Its track shone damply in the moonlight.

Gruff could see what was going to happen, but there was nothing he could do. With a crashing, crunching roar, the Weeping Stone smashed through the drystone wall between Top Field and the coast path like a bulldozer.

'Wow,' Gruff said, staring at the result. That was going to take a while to repair.

There was a deep rumble as the Weeping Stone slid down the sea wall's bank of boulders onto the beach. In the relative quiet following this, Gruff heard the odd thump and thud. Loose stones, giving up their battle with gravity. He went to inspect the damage.

It was bad. He would have to fetch a hurdle for the gaping hole, to stop the sheep from coming and having a party on the beach. The flock were currently all out of sight behind the scrubby bushes on the far side of the field but an escape route like this would not remain undiscovered for long. He felt down the sides of the hole, easing free any rocks that might fall on an unsuspecting lamb. If there was one thing lambs could be counted on to do, it was climb on top of things, and this was a particularly exciting climbing frame.

The Weeping Stone was almost there. Gruff climbed a safe section of wall and watched as it moved down the beach past its lost friends – one, two, three, four – and into the incoming sea that washed around its base in glistening peaks – five, six.

'Gruff?'

Gruff jumped and looked behind him to see Mat in a pair of blue penguin pyjamas. Her hair was tousled and her eyes sleep-confused. She stared at the destroyed wall and the rucks in the ground. 'Was that…?' she whispered.

Gruff grinned and beckoned her to climb up and join him. Mat did so without another word.

'Look,' Gruff said, pointing. Her gaze followed his finger. There was silence, and Gruff knew that Mat was counting.

'Seven,' she said quietly. She coughed. 'There's a seventh Sleeper.'

Gruff laughed into the still, moon-washed night. 'The Weeping Stone's come home.'

Chapter 26

Gruff sat by his bedroom window and waited for dawn, his old wetsuit tight beneath his jeans and jumper. Hywel lay on his feet, a furry toe-warmer. The poor old dog had been cowering silently in the hallway when Gruff got back to the farmhouse. Everyone else had slept through the noise, which was a relief, but Hywel must have not only heard the sound but sensed the strangeness of it, and it had scared him to his bones. Gruff fussed over him and let him upstairs onto his bed, which Hywel thought was a win.

Gruff himself had managed a grand total of one hour and forty-three minutes sleep. In the quiet time between moon and sun, anticipation had got the better of him. He dressed, fed the chickens, collected their eggs, brushed Hywel's coat, gave him his breakfast, and returned to his bedroom window to watch and wait for the light. A text from Mat told him that she too was awake and impatient.

HURRY UP SUN!

At last it arrived, a burst of thick orange light in a blood-red sky.

'Red sky in the morning, shepherd's warning,' Gruff murmured.

Hywel followed him downstairs and watched whilst Gruff wrote Dad and Nain a note – *Fed chickens and Hywel. Back soon*. Gruff patted Hywel goodbye, put the hammer in his rucksack and the rucksack on his back, and slipped out of the front door to find Mat standing just outside.

'Hi,' Gruff said, and they set off together for the beach.

'How long till high tide?' Mat whispered. Her voice sounded husky, her breathing heavy. Her raw new gills showed as dark slashes on her neck.

'An hour and a half,' Gruff said. He hoped it was enough time. He hadn't wanted to go out on the stones at night, but had a horrible feeling that if the tide turned before they had accomplished their task, it would be too late.

By the time they reached the head of the beach, the sky seemed to be on fire. Great bands of red and orange, broken by thin streaks of dark cloud, blazed across the eastern sky as the sun crept up from behind the far-off lumps and bumps of mainland Wales.

Dry sand slipped into Gruff's trainers as they walked down the beach. The tide was almost ten metres past the first Sleeper already, and still coming in. A high tide to match the low of the night before.

There was a difference in the Sleepers. Like the silence when a sound you have become used to stops. The wind dying. A boiler going out. A buzzing light bulb switching off.

'They're not calling,' Mat said.

'Yes.' Gruff looked out along the length of the stones. 'They're not tempting.'

They took their clothes and trainers off, down to the wetsuits, and Gruff stuffed everything in his rucksack. They waded out to the first of the Sleepers.

Mat put her hand on the stone. 'Oh … Gruff, touch it!'

Gruff placed his palm flat against the first Sleeper and contentment flooded through him, a feeling of *rightness* that twitched his mouth into a smile. 'They're happy,' he said. 'They're all together again.' Their hole of yearning was filled. No one would be lured into it now and swallowed by the sea. No more danger for Prem or Rosie or anyone else.

No more danger from the Sleepers, at any rate. Dylan was still out there, and a storm was on its way.

Mat climbed onto the first stone and Gruff followed her. They paused to dry their feet as much as possible with the towel Gruff had brought, and then put their trainers back on and set off along the Sleepers, Mat first. Beyond her, the brilliant orb of the sun cleared the horizon and spread dazzling light across the sea.

Mat already had the sword in her hand when Gruff joined her on the seventh Sleeper. She lay flat on her stomach, half hanging down towards the water. She raised the sword as he knelt beside her and the sun flashed on its turning, twisting hilt. 'Ready?' she asked. Her breathing rasped and Gruff saw with a jolt of unease that her eyes were steeped in leaping water.

The morning was very still. The sea was quiet, the wind little more than a sigh. Gruff was not sure if it was his own anticipation but the air seemed to thrum in his temples, in his veins. His sight seemed paper-thin, hyper-bright, everything in sharper focus than normal. He opened his rucksack and took the hammer from it. 'Ready', he said.

Mat plunged the sword into the sea, withdrew it and plunged it in again. She counted quietly, '*Raz, dwa, trzy, cztery, pięć, sześć, siedem*.' She eyed Gruff sideways and grinned, her ocean-filled gaze bright. 'Polish.'

Gruff grinned back. He tightened his grip on the hammer and took a steadying breath.

Mat held the sword beneath the water with both hands. Gruff leant forward and brought the ancient stone hammer round and down, breaking through the surface of the water and finally, finally connecting with the blade. A pure, sweet note ricocheted through the sea and reverberated back up his arm to sing in his bones.

Mat laughed aloud.

'*Un*,' Gruff gasped, stopping himself from bouncing up and down for joy in case he fell off the stone. He withdrew the hammer and repeated the movement, and the note rang out again. '*Dau*.' On he went, counting each blow as it fell. '*Tri, pedwar, pump, chwech, saith*.'

They were doing it. It was working.

Mat drew the sword out and thrust it down, counting again.

After its first blaze of glory, the sun was now scrambling up through thickening clouds. The wind grew. Gruff hardly noticed; he had eyes only for the hilt and the hammer and the lengthening, invisible blade. Before long he was counting in Polish and Mat was counting in Welsh and they were both giddy with hope and relief and laughter. The singing notes of hammer on blade wrapped them in a cocoon of sound that the outside world could not penetrate.

Mat tested the sword occasionally, padding along the flat of the blade to see how long it had become. 'It's narrowing,' she said, each time. 'Nearly there … we've got to be nearly there.'

Gruff struck the first blow of a set of seven and the same note rang out, but on the second a different, higher note came in harmony to the first, and on the third a deep, low note, a different one again. And on, until with the seventh blow the chord swelled around them, felt rather than heard: a chord that was almost out of harmony but holding itself together on a delicious edge of unresolved-resolved sound.

He sat back on his heels and put the hammer down, rubbing his tired arm. Mat pulled the sword up and out of the water – and the blade was there for anyone to see: long and sharp and wicked and beautiful, fluid and solid, keen and complete.

'We did it,' she whispered.

Gruff stretched one careful finger out to the blade. It was solid and dry to the touch, though it looked for all the world like flowing water.

The first drops of rain pattered to the sea around them and splashed on Gruff's cheek. He snapped his head to the sky and only then did he see the broiling, purple-black clouds covering the sun; only then did he feel the hissing excitement of the wind.

He looked back to the sword and hoped against hope that they had done enough. 'Here comes the storm.'

Chapter 27

A choppy wave slapped against the base of the seventh Sleeper and shot spray up around them. Gruff was splattered but Mat got the worst of it: it soaked her wetsuit and ran from her face in rivulets. She let the sword fall from limp fingers. It burst into water droplets and vanished into the sea.

Gruff's heart skipped a warning. 'Mat!'

Without any sign she had heard him, Mat rolled forwards onto the balls of her feet and dived into the water.

'Mat!' he screamed. He leapt for her but she was gone, swift as an eel, streaking away into the Irish Sea. The rain came harder and Gruff brushed the water from his eyes, his heart thumping with shock and adrenaline that told him to do something when nothing could be done. He couldn't swim after her. There was no way to bring her back.

She'll be fine, he told himself. *So long as she stays in her sea-state, she'll be fine.*

Unless she forgot who she was and never came back.

'Mat!' he called again, but he could see no sign of her in the heaving, slate-grey sea.

'You must try to talk to him,' a voice said in Welsh beside him, and Gruff nearly fell off the Sleeper. A hand snatched out and steadied him — the blacksmith. She gave him a quick, serious smile and Gruff saw that the raindrops plastering his hair to his head did not touch her soot-smudged face.

'You're not really here,' Gruff said.

'Not until Dylan and I are released will I be fully anywhere,' the blacksmith said. 'But you and I are both standing on the threshold. Can't you feel it?'

'Threshold?' Gruff was lost.

'In the air. You must feel it.'

Gruff stared around. In the air. Did she mean this electric feeling, where everything felt fresh and clear and hyper-real? He had thought it was his own excitement, but perhaps there was more to it than that. It had affected Mat too. She had been full of the sea as soon as she had stepped onto the seventh Sleeper. She must have held the feeling back like a coiled spring throughout the blade-forging, right up until that wave hit her and she could resist no longer.

'Can you help me get Mat back?' he asked.

'Mat?'

'She held the sword.'

211

'Oh, the morgen.'

'The – wait, what?' Something stirred in Gruff's memory. Something Nain had said, when she sang him the song about the Sleepers being a bridge. Something about a morgen being like a mermaid? 'A mermaid?' he asked.

'Morgens are merpeople, yes.'

'Don't mermaids have tails?' Gruff said, wondering with alarm if that was going to be the next stage for Mat.

'No tails,' the blacksmith smiled. 'They have scales, and gills, and webbed hands and feet, and an incredible strength at swimming. But you know what they look like. You saw Dylan.'

'So Mat *is* like Dylan.' Gruff bit his lip. 'Does that mean she'll stop living on land?'

'If she chooses. The potential for full transformation comes if a morgen reaches the point of drowning. Most just live their lives as very good human swimmers.'

The point of drowning. The blacksmith's words dripped cold down Gruff's spine. If Mat hadn't been a morgen, she would have drowned that night she leapt off the Sleepers. And he would have drowned trying to save her.

Spray splattered Gruff's legs. He became suddenly

acutely aware of where they were standing. 'We can't stay here,' he said, above the wind. 'We've got to get to shore.'

'No,' the blacksmith snapped. 'We have to talk to Dylan – *you* have to talk to him. I cannot. He doesn't hear me or see me except when we play out our parts, and that will be very soon now. Once it begins, I can't talk to you, and you can't reach Dylan. Do you understand?'

'No.' He was sick of not understanding.

The blacksmith kneaded her hands together, increasingly agitated. 'I'm stuck in between, neither here nor there, and so is Dylan. I didn't kill him that day but nor can he heal. I can't help, and I can't cross the threshold!'

Gruff staggered in the wind. 'What threshold?! To what?'

'We're on it. Here, on the edge of the land and the sea, the layers of life between this world and Annwn are thin. All magic is stronger and even mortals can pass across.'

'What's Annwn?'

'The otherworld. The immortal realm.'

'The otherworld?' Gruff's reality expanded uncomfortably. 'Like in Nain and Taid's old stories?'

A threshold between worlds. No wonder Mat had

been drawn to her magical side. And that must be why the sword had to be forged from this stone.

Seven Sleepers on the sea, bridging is their work.

A bridge to the otherworld of myth and legend.

'I can help you call Dylan,' the blacksmith said. 'I taught others in the past, before the bridge was broken by a man who hoped to stop contact with the otherworld. He didn't realise what a terrible mistake he was making. He didn't foresee the storms the island would suffer without any way to reach Dylan and calm him. Since then even fewer people have been able to see me, and only then at times of great danger.'

Speaking to Dylan might calm him? Might stop the storm? Gruff planted his feet firmly and scrubbed his eyes free of rain. 'What do I need to do?'

'To call him, you must say: *Dylan Ail Don, ni thorrodd don o dano erioed; a wnewch chi siarad â mi?*'

Dylan Ail Don, beneath whom no wave ever breaks; will you speak with me?

'I hope he comes,' the blacksmith added, almost to herself. 'If he's too lost in his pain, he won't hear. This storm is set to be one of the worst we've seen. The conditions are as they were that terrible day.' She took a small step backwards so Gruff stood alone. 'If the storm can't be stopped, remember the sword.'

'What does it do?'

214

'If you have forged it well,' the blacksmith said, 'it should cut water.'

Gruff half laughed. 'What? Anything can cut through water. It's water! It's not solid!'

'The sword doesn't cut *through* water: it cuts water,' the blacksmith snapped. 'We're running out of time. Call him. Please.'

Gruff squinted out into the choppy waves. His mind filled with the memory of cold, webbed fingers tearing at his own, trying to wrench the hammer from his grasp. But then he remembered the Dylan he had seen in the played-out past, the Dylan before the hammer strike. The curious Dylan who had swum towards the beautiful sword-forging music, fearing no harm.

Could that Dylan still be there, underneath the anger and pain?

'*Dylan Ail Don, ni thorrodd don o dano erioed; a wnewch chi siarad â mi?*' Gruff shouted, in as clear a voice as he could. The wind threw his words into the sky and smashed them against the waves. For a long minute the rain pattered down and the spray splashed up and nothing broke the surface of the sea.

A movement, right beside the rock – but it was only a cormorant, bobbing up to swallow its catch. A kittiwake skimmed low past the seventh Sleeper, buffeted by the wind. The cormorant dived again, hunting for pudding.

Gruff thought he saw Mat's dark head appear far away to the right, but the next second he realised it was just a seal. His heart thumped hard. He should be out looking for her – but how?

Still no Dylan. Should he say the words again? He half turned back to the blacksmith but she whispered, '*Arhoswch.*' Wait. So he waited, and tried not to think about how long it had been since Mat dived into the sea.

A head surfaced close in front of him.

Dull, grey scales, dark slashes of gills, human eyes imbued with a swollen sea.

Dylan Ail Don had come at Gruff's call.

Chapter 28

This was not the curious, carefree Dylan who had swum into the blacksmith's hammer strike, nor the terrifying Dylan who had borne down on Gruff and Mat with such pain-filled anger. This Dylan looked sad and tired.

His sunken cheeks and the hollows around his eyes showed the curves of his skull. His lips were thin, cracked lines. His eyes held a sea that was heavy and turgid; a pre-storm sea. On his chest was a deep, congealed wound, lined with torn scales and broken bone. The dark brown-black of old blood mingled with the shine of oil, and scraps of a plastic bag and an old fishing net were embedded in the half-healed, never-closed wound. It smelled horrible; the sweet stench of decay. Dylan's drawn face was that of a person so used to pain they cannot remember a time before it.

Gruff didn't know what to do or say. When he glanced behind him he found himself alone. The blacksmith was gone.

'I...' Gruff crouched down on the Sleeper so that

he was closer to Dylan. Rain pattered down around them. The morgen bobbed in the swell, which seemed calmer around the rock, though Gruff could see the waves were still wild beyond.

What could he say? Please don't swamp the island? Please take your anger and pain out into the middle of the ocean, far away?

When he spoke, what Gruff actually found himself saying was: '*Dw i isio helpu chi.*' I want to help you.

Dylan's cracked lips parted and a layered sound came out, a low groan beneath a strange breathy whistle.

'Um…' Gruff said, unsure whether this noise was a good or bad sign. Was this morgen language? Could Dylan not speak with a human voice?

Dylan slowly raised one arm – his right arm, the side without the wound – towards Gruff. His fingers were long and thin and joined with webbing that had once been sturdy but was now ragged and raw.

Did he want Gruff to shake his hand? Gruff paused to see if Dylan would do or say anything else. He did not, so Gruff leant down and placed his hand into Dylan's in the strangest handshake ever. Dylan's fingers were cold, but not slimy like he'd imagined. The morgen's grip was firm. It sent a wash of water up Gruff's arm, calmer than what he sensed from Mat.

'No one,' Dylan said, in a voice as ragged as his hand, 'has spoken to me in a long time.' He let Gruff's hand go and dropped back down into the water so that his gills were covered. When he spoke again, his voice was a little less hoarse. 'Did Gofannon teach you to call me?'

Gruff hesitated. He had never asked the blacksmith's name. Was she Gofannon? 'The blacksmith showed me how. She's really sorry. She never meant to hurt you.'

Dylan's lips pulled down and his teeth flashed in a grimace. 'I do not blame her. We are as cursed as one another.'

'How can I help?' Gruff asked. 'Please, tell me how!'

'I'm sorry. I cannot tell you what I do not know.'

'Then why has she shown me how to talk to you? I don't know what to do!'

'You are doing everything you can,' Dylan said. 'I am … talking. I see you. We have taken hands. The more I remember of what I once was, the less dangerous I will be when I am not myself.'

Gruff's heart sank. 'So that's it? The storm'll happen, but it might not be as bad as it could've been?'

'I'm … so sorry.' Dylan's face twisted and he began to turn away.

219

'No! Please stay.' Gruff searched for something to say. Something to keep Dylan talking and remembering. 'My friend is a morgen, I think. She's got gills.'

A spark of interest flashed in Dylan's tired eyes. 'A morgen? There hasn't been another here for many years. Will she choose the water?'

'I … don't know.' Gruff remembered his conversation with Mat in the farmhouse kitchen, how she had told him that being in the sea was like coming home. 'Will you please look out for her?' he said. 'She swam away, it's like she's forgotten who she is.'

'She must forget to discover,' Dylan said. 'The memories will return. Eventually.'

'Eventually?'

'It can take some years.'

Gruff's stomach turned over. Losing Mat. That's what it would be, if she turned full morgen. Her family would lose her. He would lose her. She would be gone. Mat had said she felt *hiraeth* for the sea. Would she really leave and not look back?

'Mat's learning to be an oceanographer,' he said. 'She's going to be a really good one.' *Don't go, Mat.*

Dylan turned full circle in the water, scanning the waves. 'I will look out for her.' He frowned. 'So long as I am myself. So long as I remember.'

Gruff's eyes were drawn again to the terrible, rubbish-filled wound. 'Let me help,' he said. 'Maybe I can get some of that stuff out?'

Dylan flinched away as though Gruff had been about to touch him, though Gruff had not moved. 'There is nothing you can do. I am immortal, and yet I have a mortal wound. It will never heal. If you touch it … the pain that would cause … I could drown you. Not from choice, but it would happen. Do you understand? I … forget myself.'

Gruff drew his knees up and wrapped his arms around them, shivering in the rain. He felt useless. 'We do beach litter-picking all the time here,' he said. 'I'm sorry the sea is so full of rubbish.'

'You apologise on behalf of your species.'

'I suppose so, yeah.'

The hammer caught Gruff's eye, lying on the rock next to him. He picked it up and turned it over in his hand absent-mindedly. 'How can a sword cut water?' he asked. 'And how does that help in a storm?'

Dylan made a choking noise and Gruff looked up in alarm. The morgen's eyes were trained on the hammer. His thin lips drew back and Gruff saw that Dylan's teeth ended in sharp points, like those of a seal. A high, whistling hiss erupted from his chest, his teeth parting and the rain glinting on those terrible canines.

'I won't hurt you!' Gruff yelped, leaping to his feet and taking a step back. He held the hammer behind him, out of sight, but the damage was done.

Dylan dived beneath the waves with the scream of a wounded animal and a great leap of water burst up, battering Gruff with stinging droplets.

The bubble of calm was gone. The wind and rain and spray hit Gruff with full fury and he saw a great wave on its way, pulsing up from below as though there had been an eruption underwater. Dylan was frightened and angry, and the sea was responding.

Abandoning his rucksack, Gruff turned and leapt for the sixth Sleeper as the explosion of water roared down behind him. He retreated as fast as he could, jumping from stone to stone, his trainers slipping on the slick, soaked surfaces. The rain pummelled him from above and the sea clawed from below.

Gruff splashed down onto the sand of the beach, water up to his chest. The swell tried to knock him off his feet, but he set himself firm and waded through it. The water was at his waist and then his knees and then his ankles, and finally he was out and running on rain-soaked sand. Only when he reached the great gash in the sea wall, caused by the passing of the seventh Sleeper, did he turn and look back out to the stones. He saw the blacksmith, crouching there, and she held in her hand something that glinted even in the dull grey storm-light.

It was the sword hilt.

It was beginning again.

Gofannon the blacksmith and Dylan Ail Don the morgen, trapped in time and forced to relive a terrible accident. Dylan would receive his wound once more.

But this time the storm had already begun.

Chapter 29

Gruff squinted at the scene on the seventh Sleeper, holding tight to the hammer in his hand. He'd done as the blacksmith asked and talked to Dylan, but had he just made everything worse? He wished he hadn't let Dylan see the hammer.

He watched the blacksmith raise her own hammer and bring it down. The waves roared about her but she did not seem to see or feel them in her in-between world.

'Gruff!' Nain was stumbling along the coast path, wearing her grey raincoat and shockingly yellow sou'wester hat. 'Why are you in a wetsuit? Tell me you haven't been out on those stones! Tell me you haven't –' She broke off and stared at the deep track cutting through the field and stone wall and path before her. 'What on earth…?' She turned to the beach and Gruff saw her eyes flicking as she counted. 'There's seven,' she said faintly.

'Yeah,' Gruff said. 'Have you seen Mat?'

'What? No, not today. She's not really an early riser, is she?'

'Not usually,' he mumbled. He had to get to Mat's house and see if she'd returned without him. He hoped so.

'But … how are there seven? Oh!' Understanding lit up her eyes. 'The Weeping Stone?'

'Yes. It moved itself.' Gruff clambered up the steep sea wall to the path, wanting to be away.

'Well, there's no hiding that,' Nain said, nodding at the dark muddy river running down Top Field through the Weeping Stone's track. 'Now even the most sceptical will have to start believing in the legends! Though I'm thinking Ffion will be the hardest to convince. She'll tell us that was made by an abnormally large mole.'

Gruff snorted with laughter despite himself. Nain was right. That was exactly what Ffion would say.

The wind gusted and Nain staggered.

'What are you doing out here?' Gruff scolded. 'This is just the beginning. You've got to get under cover.'

'You're one to talk!' she squawked. 'For your information I'm on my way to the fishermen's cottages. Some of them haven't seen a Wounded Sea storm before and they might not know what best to do. Iolo always keeps sandbags for twenty houses in his shed. He and I will make sure they're put out where they need to be.'

'I'll come later,' Gruff said. 'I've got to see if Mat's okay.'

Her eyes narrowed. 'Why shouldn't she be? What were you doing out on those forsaken stones?'

'Later, Nain,' Gruff pleaded. 'I'm sorry – but please, later?'

'Later.' Nain sniffed. 'I'll hold you to that.' She tightened the string of the sou'wester under her chin and ploughed on, splashing through the deep gouge cut by the Weeping Stone. Gruff ran in the other direction, the wind blowing him away from the sea towards Blacksmith's Cottage – and, he hoped desperately, Mat.

He came into the farmyard just as Dad appeared from the sheep barn, running. Gruff heard the shrill beeping of the lifeboat pager Dad carried with him at all times, and his heart rocked in his chest. He hated this. Every time. He hated it.

As he ran past, Dad yelled over his shoulder, 'Batten down the hatches, Gruff. Be safe!'

'No!' Gruff tried to shout the word but it came out as a cracked sound, and Dad was already in Top Field, haring across it towards the lifeboat station.

Then there was another running shape: Zosia, hastily dressed in leggings and a T-shirt, already drenched, racing after Dad.

'Not in this storm,' Gruff whispered. Red-hot panic roiled in his chest and anger flashed at whoever had got into trouble out there. Just as quickly, guilt dampened the anger. Of course the lifeboat had to go.

But … *this* storm. Dad out in the boat in *this* storm. A supernatural storm.

A supernatural storm that Gruff might have made worse.

Mat wasn't at home. John answered the door looking dishevelled and sick, and said he'd thought Mat was with Gruff. Gruff said maybe she was with Iolo, crossing his fingers tightly behind his back and wishing he could tell John the truth. John was drumming his hand against his thigh without seeming to realise he was doing it, and his eyes kept flicking to the heaving sea. Gruff remembered something Mat had said – that after Zosia met John they had moved to Manchester, far away from the sea. Was this the first time John had seen Zosia run into a storm?

'They're a really good crew,' Gruff said, as John was closing the door. John paused and looked at Gruff properly. 'The lifeboat crew,' Gruff explained. 'And Zosia's experience is brilliant, Dad said. And she's done her top-up training. So … they're … all as prepared as they should be.' It felt odd to be reassuring an adult he hardly knew.

John stared at him as though he had never seen Gruff before in his life. Then a tiny, anxious smile flicked the corner of his mouth. 'Does it get any less frightening? When they go?'

Gruff swallowed painfully. 'No. Sorry.'

'Good lad.' John placed one hand on Gruff's shoulder, and seemed to notice the wetsuit for the first time. 'You're not going swimming!'

'No, don't worry! See you later.'

Gruff beat a hasty retreat to the farmhouse and James and Ffion hailed him as he reached the front door. They were walking towards him across the yard in full waterproofs and wellington boots, grinning widely, Ffion's blonde hair plastered to her face and raindrops shining in James's tight black curls. Old Hywel trotted between them.

'Gruff, I like the wetsuit idea!' James laughed. 'I should have done that.'

'We've finished getting the sheep into the barn,' Ffion said. 'It's too soon after shearing for them to get soaked and frozen in this. The hens are shut up too. Your dad says you're to stay inside.'

'This is a proper Wounded Sea storm,' James grinned, pumped up on the energy of the weather itself. 'I've never seen one like it.'

'And the Weeping Stone!' Ffion added. 'Have you

seen what's happened, Gruff? It's been moved! It's out on the end of the Sleepers now! Who moved it?'

'It moved itself,' Gruff said, managing to get a word in edgeways. He was glad the sheep were in. That was one less thing to worry about. He bent down and patted Hywel's soggy head. Hywel pushed his nose into Gruff's palm and gazed at him with eyes that said *I'm far too old for this palaver.*

'I knew it!' James cried. 'I told you, Ffi!'

'Rubbish,' Ffion said amiably. 'It's a lot of effort for a prank though!'

'Look, Gruff,' James said, 'we're just going to the fishermen's cottages to check everyone's all right. Stay inside, okay? Keep Hywel with you.'

Gruff made a non-committal noise but luckily James and Ffion must have taken it as positive, because they signed at Hywel to stay and set off for the fishermen's cottages.

Hywel sat and stared up at Gruff. '*Tyrd,*' Gruff said. Come. He opened the farmhouse door and Hywel leapt joyfully inside and gave himself an almighty shake. Gruff grabbed the towel they kept hanging on the coat pegs and rubbed Hywel down before pointing to the living room. 'You can even get on the sofa if you want,' he said. 'There's no one here to tell you off.' Hywel didn't need any more encouragement.

He bounded like a puppy into the living room and Gruff heard the creak of springs as the old dog leapt onto the even older sofa.

Gruff left the relative calm of the farmhouse – where the wind was whistling round the corners and down the chimney and the rain was splattering the windows – and entered the full force of the storm once again. He had to try and find Mat.

He had not gone more than two steps when a loud crack shot through the sound of the wind and rain. He ducked instinctively, his arms crossed above his head. He had lived through enough storms to know the sound of something breaking under pressure.

Thankfully, no blow came – but the bleating of the sheep seemed to get much louder. 'Oh no,' Gruff muttered.

Panicked white, brown and grey-and-black blobs started legging it across the yard and down into Bottom Field. 'Not that way!' Gruff yelled. He raced across the yard and blocked the entrance to the barn where the door had been newly ripped from its hinges and lay broken on the ground. Four-legged bodies barrelled into him, the sheep terrified and wanting to just run. Gruff set himself low and firm and blocked their escape till they cowered back in the semi-darkness, all glittering eyes and fearful bleating.

Gruff thought quickly. This was still the safest place for the flock, so long as he could keep them in. The spare hurdles were stacked just to the right of the door – he lunged sideways to grab one, and a ewe and her twins dashed past through the gap. He dragged the hurdle across the entrance on the inside and jumped over so that he was in with the sheep. He found some twine and secured the hurdle tightly. Then he turned and did the fastest head-count he'd ever done.

Seventy-four sheep, six lambs. He'd lost thirty-eight sheep and seven lambs to the storm.

Ffion would have her walkie-talkie on her. Gruff ran back to the house and searched for Dad's, eventually finding it on the mantelpiece. Hywel watched him from the sofa with the pricked ears of a dog who can sense that break-time is nearly over.

Gruff clicked to Ffion's channel and pressed the 'talk' button. 'Hello? The barn door's blown off; half the flock's loose in Bottom Field. Hello?'

Nothing. He tried Iolo, then Deepa and Hardik. He tried ringing out on his mobile. Perhaps the storm was disrupting the calls, or they were all too busy fighting the waves to notice the crackle of their walkie-talkies or ringing of their phones.

Gruff closed his eyes. The sheep were out there,

caught in the wild weather. A Wounded Sea storm like the one that had claimed half the flock when Nain was little. It mustn't happen again. Not to his flock.

'Hywel!'

Hywel poked his nose rebelliously under the sofa cushion.

'I'm sorry,' Gruff said. 'Really. I'll make sure you get chicken for this. *Tyrd*.'

Hywel might have been a disappointed sheep dog but he was a loyal one. He trotted after Gruff, a martyr resigned to his fate.

'All right, Hywel,' Gruff said to him as they ventured out into the yard. 'Let's go get these sheep.'

Chapter 30

Bottom Field was awash with seawater and sheep.

It was only their first, terrified, headlong rush that had brought them within reach of the waves, but now they were there it was impossible to escape. The boggy grass was as treacherous as quicksand. As the sheep struggled to retreat, towering breakers battered them off their hooves and swept them bleating into the flood.

Gruff's world teetered. The shape of the coast he had known all his life was lost in a new tideline that ate half of Bottom Field up in one gulp and clawed hungrily for more. His mind was blank and he could not begin to work out how to help the terrified flock. Then Hywel nuzzled his hand and the old dog's touch seemed to ground him. Gruff remembered Dad's lessons and imagined the field and the sheep as a puzzle to be solved. He saw the paths that Hywel needed to take, and he brought his rainwater-wet fingers to his mouth and whistled. Hywel sped into the fray, mud flinging in clods from his paws.

Gruff got Hywel to work slowly down the field, gradually collecting the sheep as though they were cream being skimmed off the top of fresh milk from Evan's cows. Hywel came round again and again, corralling the frightened sheep, persuading them up the slope towards the farmhouse, then dashing back for the next pass until there were over twenty runaways huddled around Gruff.

Gruff whistled Hywel back down for the next group and, too late, saw a wave sweeping low and deadly along the ground towards the old dog. It carried Hywel and the sheep he had gone to collect right off their feet, washing them up the field and back down to the sea, faster than thought.

'No!' Gruff screamed.

Hywel and the sheep floundered in a mess of heads and legs and Gruff lost sight of them as the next wave thundered over.

Gruff ran down the field with no real idea of what to do. As he reached the place where Hywel had fallen, he saw the old dog labouring on the crest of a new wave, black-and-white fur clinging close to his bones and his eyes utterly trusting as they met Gruff's. Gruff braced himself and the wave thumped into his knees; he caught Hywel as he swept up to him, and clung to him tightly as the water ebbed back. Then he was stumbling up the slope, carrying Hywel awkwardly in his arms, half sobbing with relief.

As Gruff reached the huddled flock, Hywel licked his face and struggled to get down. Gruff put him on the grass and the old dog shook himself so determinedly that he almost fell over. Gruff steadied him and looked back the way they had come. His stomach turned at the sight of the sheep still tossing in the edges of the storm-capped sea. 'I'll come back,' he whispered.

Right now he had to do something about the shivering flock too confused to move further up the field, and the drenched dog who had nearly drowned for his loyalty. 'Walk up,' he whistled, and Hywel padded ahead of him on shaky legs, encouraging the sheep towards the farmyard. Gruff counted them as they walked. Twenty-seven ewes and wethers, four lambs. Baa-bara's two lambs were missing. She was the most distressed of the group, bleating loudly and trying to turn back. Gruff felt sick with guilt. 'I'll look for them,' he said. 'I promise.' Though he did not hold high hopes of finding them in that wide, wild sea.

They entered the farmyard and Gruff went ahead and untied the twine, opening his makeshift barrier into the barn. Hywel brought up the rear, seeing the rescued runaways safely inside.

Gruff secured the hurdle and ran to the farmhouse, Hywel loping behind him. He unlatched the door and ushered Hywel inside. 'Good boy. Good boy. You're the best of dogs.' He rubbed him down with the already-damp towel, rewarded him with a handful of treats and left him on the sofa, wrapped in a blanket. Then he grabbed a coil of rope from the tool shed and ran back to Bottom Field.

The rain had stopped whilst he was inside the farmhouse but the spray on the wind was so thick that it hardly seemed to make a difference. His hands were freezing but his adrenaline burnt like fire inside him. Eleven sheep and three lambs, two of them separated from their mother. He had to try.

He had to.

Gruff headed straight for the single, windswept hawthorn tree growing in the middle of Bottom Field. He looped the rope under his armpits as he ran, squelching towards waves that were taller than him. He reached the hawthorn and grabbed its gnarled bark just as a wave broke over the top of him, filling his eyes and nose with brine. He coughed and clung there until the water had subsided, working itself up for its next attack. With fumbling fingers Gruff tied the end of the rope round a branch, using a boat knot Dai had taught him. He tugged once on it and ran on down the field, scraping his eyes free of water and squinting through the spray.

Ahead of him he saw Dave and Greta half staggering, half swimming through deep water, Greta nudging her limp lamb ahead of her with anxious bleats. Gruff waded forwards and grabbed the lamb in both arms. She had always been half the size of the other lambs and was so weak now she hardly tried to struggle, but Gruff could feel her heart beating hard against his hands as he turned and led the way out of the water. Spurred on by this apparent kidnap attempt, Greta splashed after him until they were both free of the sea and staggering up the boggy field, Dave right behind them. Gruff put the lamb down and she immediately fell over. Greta nuzzled her and Gruff dithered, wondering if he should take them all the way up to the farm – but the sheep and lambs still out there didn't have the luxury of time.

Gruff turned, tripped over his own rope and slid back down into the waves. He pushed himself to his feet and called into the wind. '*Defaid! Deeefaid!*' Sheep! He stopped and listened ... and a bleat came from somewhere to his left. Gruff waded until he ran out of land and then swam, the rope under his arms both a burden and a reassurance.

The bleat had belonged to silver-backed Bess, and to Gruff's joy he saw that she was with Baabara's two lost lambs. They were all doggy-paddling valiantly towards him out of the mist of spray. Gruff scooped his arm round Bess's back-end, pushing her onwards, and with his free hand did his best to help the lambs stay afloat as he kicked his legs and headed for shore.

The small, dripping group he had left at the top of the field had swelled to five adults by the time Gruff arrived with Bess and her entourage. 'How did you get here?' Gruff laughed, giving Seren, Lewis and Frank relieved rubs on their backs and checking on Greta's lamb. 'Well done, guys!'

He ran back down the field, hope shining in his heart. Five more to find. He might actually make it! He might actually get them all to safety...

A scream of pain split the air. The sea swelled and came crashing onto the land with the pure anger of agony. It carried Gruff with it out into open water, well beyond the edge of the field. He struggled for the surface and gasped for breath, the rope drawing tight around his chest. The water here was colder, deeper, the island invisible beyond a curtain of spray. The scream had become a roar and melded with the sound of the wind and the sea.

It had happened. Dylan was struck. A wound upon his wound.

Dad's out in this, Gruff thought. *And Mat. And her*

mum. And everyone else on the lifeboat, and whoever they've gone to help.

He shuddered in the deep, cold water and forced his mind back to the sheep.

Gruff was lucky the tide was only just on the turn, or he might not have bumped into Fiona and Cai as they were swept back towards the land with the next wave. He grabbed them and helped them swim to safety. His arms and legs shook with the cold and strain as he turned once again for the water.

The wind dipped, just for a moment, and the spray cleared. In that second Gruff saw three struggling bodies far out to sea, caught by the current. The last three sheep. Guinevere, he recognised even from this distance. Bile rose in his throat. The sea had taken them away from him. They would drown. They would drown and there was nothing he could do.

As he stood there, wretched in that absolute certainty, a wave took him from his feet. The rope pulled taut, the tree branch snapped and he was released to the mercy of the sea.

Chapter 31

Gruff twisted his body round and began to swim grimly back towards the land. He felt the current pull at his legs and knew he had to keep moving or it would sweep him away like it had taken the sheep. He tried not to think about them, or the huddled group he had left at the top of the field, or Dad and Zosia and the rest of the lifeboat crew, or Mat. He tried not to think about what would happen if the current claimed him. *Just keep swimming*, he thought.

A tug on the rope. For a moment he thought it was just the loose end catching against something, but then three tugs came in quick succession and with a rush of relief he realised that someone had found him. James? Ffion? Nain? He wrapped numb fingers round the cord and tugged back. There was a pause, and then Gruff was jerking through the water in short spurts, the rope tight under his arms as someone reeled him in hand over hand.

The water warmed and Gruff found land beneath his feet. He staggered up the field to find that his rescuer was John, a pile of rope beside him and his face red with exertion.

'Thank you,' Gruff gasped, as John untied the swollen rope from round his chest.

'What the hell do you think you're doing?' John's voice was hoarse with fear and anger. 'If I hadn't come down the field –'

'The barn door broke,' Gruff said wretchedly. 'I was looking for them. I lost three sheep. I failed.'

'Oh, Gruff...' John glanced at the huddle of bedraggled animals. 'You were rescuing your sheep?' He put one waterproofed arm round Gruff's shoulders. 'Let's get you and this lot back to the farm. Then I'm going to the fishermen's cottages to find Mat. You said she'd gone to see Iolo?' He shuddered. 'Did you hear that horrible screaming sound? I thought maybe you were hurt; I went to the farmhouse and when you weren't there I came looking... This storm is worse than I realised, and I don't even know where Mat is...' His voice broke.

'Gruff! John!'

Gruff's heart leapt. That was Mat's voice! He and John turned as one and ran back down the field. Mat was headed for shore on the crest of a wave, and with her...

'Hetty!' Gruff waded in and grabbed the sheep

from Mat, hauling her up so she could get her feet on solid ground.

John splashed into the water. 'It's all right, Matty, I've got you.'

'No! I can't –'

John picked her up out of the water and Mat gasped and clawed at him, and then at her throat. Gruff leapt forwards, realising what must be happening. 'John! She can't breathe!'

'What?' Shock at Mat's panic etched deep lines across John's face.

Gruff lifted one of Mat's plaits away from her neck so that John could see the raw flaps of skin there. John made a small choking noise in his throat. 'What's happened?' he whispered. 'Did you cut yourself on the rocks?'

But Mat couldn't speak and Gruff saw that she was losing air. She was a fish out of water, gasping for life.

'Put her back in the sea!' Gruff shouted. 'Please, John. She's a morgen. She's got gills. Put her back in the sea or she can't breathe!'

'What?' John was close to tears, and so confused that Gruff knew there was no way to persuade him without showing him the truth of it. He grabbed John's hands and loosened them, pulling him away so that Mat dropped into the water like a limp rag doll. She slipped under the surface and John lunged towards her, but Gruff hung onto his arm. 'No! I promise it's okay. It's okay.'

Mat bobbed back up, fresh as a daisy. 'I'm fine,' she said. 'I'm sorry, John. I've got to go back – there's two more sheep out there.'

'Mat … thank you…' Gruff watched as she sped away through the waves, which seemed somehow smoother where she passed.

'But,' John whispered, 'Mat can't swim.'

'Um,' Gruff said. 'I wish Mat had told you all this before. But she was worried what you'd think.'

John blinked at him and then jumped as Mat reappeared with a soggy sheep in tow and handed her over before speeding away again. 'Why don't *you* tell me?' he suggested. 'Whatever it is, I've got no choice but to believe it.'

Mat was back again, impossibly fast, and Guinevere trotted ashore as cheerfully as if she'd just been for a short paddle in the stream rather than a long slog through the Irish Sea. She shook herself off and bounded away up the field. 'What a ridiculously lucky sheep,' Gruff said. He turned to Mat, bobbing in the shallows. The waves were quieter around her and though the spray leapt wildly high to either side, it hardly touched them here. Gruff was reminded of the bubble of calm around Dylan.

'Thank you *so much*,' Gruff said. 'And I'm really glad you know who you are, even though you're swimming.'

Mat didn't meet his eyes. 'I don't think I can come ashore.'

'Dylan said it's your choice,' Gruff said firmly.

Mat's mouth dropped open. 'You talked to Dylan? Did you find out what the sword is for?'

'Who's Dylan? What sword?' John squeaked.

'I can make the waves calmer by thinking calmly when I'm swimming through them,' Mat said, not waiting for Gruff to answer and ignoring John completely. 'I didn't know until I went to get the sheep. I was trying to calm them down by being calm, and the waves got less so it was easier for them to swim. I've got to go out to the lifeboat and do that.'

'What?!' John exploded. 'You're not going back out there! Even if you can swim, which I don't understand, you could be crushed by the boat. Matylda, please –'

'If you were me, John, I know you'd go and help them,' Mat said. 'I love you and Mama. See you later.' And she was gone, before anyone could say another word.

She left her question behind, unanswered. *Did you find out what the sword is for?*

Yes. Gruff *had* found out what the sword was for. If the blacksmith was right, it was for cutting water.

Gruff hadn't even thought of the sword in his panic for the sheep. He couldn't see how it would have helped him, anyway. How was cutting water some kind of magic power? Water was water. Anything could cut through it. But then again, the first time he had seen the blacksmith, her words to him had been 'Finish it, or he'll kill us all'. Which meant that now the sword was finished, they stood some chance against Dylan.

There had to be something he was missing.

Gruff dropped to his knees in the shallow water and plunged his right arm in above his elbow. He closed his eyes and felt around, buffeted by wind and spray.

There it was, cold and solid against his palm. He wrapped his fingers around the sword hilt, a thrill of trepidation running through him. What if it just disintegrated when he drew it from the sea? He had never succeeded before.

'What are you doing?' John snapped. 'We've got to get out of here.' He broke off with a yelp. 'Wave! Big wave! Move *now*!'

Gruff pulled his hand up and out of the water. The sword followed in an arc of droplets, the fluid-solid blade flashing bright even on this dull day. The sea animals on the hilt wriggled and writhed against Gruff's fingers.

'Sword!' John goggled. He grabbed Gruff's elbow and dragged him away as a great rush of water chased them up the field. The wave caught their ankles and swept ahead of them before turning and racing back towards the sea. Struggling in the foaming water, captured in the wave's attack, was a weak, half-drowned scrap of bedraggled black fleece. Greta's lamb.

Gruff leapt towards the lamb but she was too far away and the water would carry her out of reach before he could get there. He threw out his sword-arm, thinking to catch the lamb against the flat of the blade and hold her there. The sword sliced through the water – and the wave split in two.

The greater part of it rushed on, back towards the sea, but the wave's foaming fringe fizzed and swirled aimlessly, its power gone. The lamb staggered to her feet as the remnants of the wave bubbled down into the sodden grass.

Gruff raised the sword up and stared at it.

If you have forged it well, it should cut water.

Another wave swept towards them. Gruff grabbed the lamb tightly and turned to meet it, slashing the sword back and forth across the water as it reached his toes. The wave continued on and up to either side of him but at his feet the sword-cuts stopped it short and it fizzled away back into the sea. Gruff laughed out loud at the complete strangeness of it all.

'Impossible,' John croaked.

Gruff grinned. 'Awesome.' Now he understood why the blacksmith had wanted them to finish the sword. It was a defence against the sea.

There was a loud crackle of static and John pulled a walkie-talkie out of his coat pocket. 'I saw it on your boot-rack,' he said apologetically. 'I thought I might need it.'

The walkie-talkie crackled again and Iolo's voice blurted from it.

'Gruff. Matylda. Are you receiving? There's something in these waves. It's Dylan, isn't it? He's trying to drown us. He's giving the storm purpose. He's angry.'

John looked at Gruff in silence.

'Yeah, it's Dylan,' Gruff said. 'And Iolo's right. He's really angry. And hurt.'

Iolo's voice crackled again. 'Matylda? Gruff? Did you manage to finish the sword? I don't know what to do.'

Gruff tightened his grip on the sword, plucked the walkie-talkie from John's hand and pressed the 'talk' button. 'Iolo? I'm coming.'

Chapter 32

Gruff and John ran across Top Field towards the fishermen's cottages, hardly visible through the whipped spray, waves biting at their lime-washed stones. When they were halfway there James raced past in the opposite direction, having received Gruff's radioed message to Iolo about the salt-encrusted sheep and half-brine lambs huddled in the barn.

'Gruff!' James gasped. 'You've got a *sword*!'

'Yes,' Gruff said, in too much of a rush to explain. 'Greta's lamb is really bad, and Hetty's wheezing like a broken bicycle pump.'

'Well done for getting them out,' James said. 'The worst danger now'll be pneumonia. I'll do everything I can.' He shuddered. 'Be careful out there – there's something in the water. I've felt its hands on me.'

The track scored through the field by the seventh Sleeper had become a raging river. Gruff took it at a run and a jump, but he came down hard just within the trench, mud up to his ankles and water up to his knees. He stumbled but managed not to let go of the sword. John's longer legs brought him safely to land

and he turned and pulled Gruff free of the clagging, sucking earth. As Gruff found his balance, he caught a glimpse of bright, brave orange in the angry grey sea. It was the lifeboat, so far out he couldn't even see the boat they had gone to assist.

Gruff turned away with an effort and ran on. There was nothing he could do. Mat was out there. Mat would help them.

The fishermen's cottages were a mess. Rosie's had lost half of its shingled roof and several of Tim's windows were broken. The bank of boulders at the head of the beach was just visible above a swollen sea. Garden walls were little more than piles of rubble. Jack and Dafydd's front door had been torn away and water now washed across the flagged floor inside. Exhausted flood-fighters swept water away from front steps and re-stacked sandbags: Gruff saw Hardik and Deepa, Ffion, Tim from the wool crew, Jack and Dafydd, Nain, Rosie, and a man and woman Gruff recognised as the bed and breakfast guests staying with Hardik and Deepa. The woman was helping the man in through Hardik and Deepa's front door; he was limping badly, his face screwed up in pain.

Hardik waved his broom over his head when he saw Gruff and John splashing through the shin-deep water. 'We've been trying to keep it out of the houses but it's impossible,' he gasped as another wave pummelled them. 'We're going to have to evacuate.'

'Where's Iolo?' Gruff asked.

'With Elen and the babies,' Deepa replied, heaving a sandbag back into position. 'He was hit by a falling shingle, but Elen's patching him up.'

Ffion waded towards them, clutching another broom. 'I think I'll have to believe Iolo's stories, Gruff,' she said grimly. 'I've seen a face in the water today – and it wasn't human.'

'*Gruffydd ap Owain!*' Gruff turned to see Nain bearing down on him with as much fearsome fury as the sea itself. '*What* are you doing here? Get back home, this instant!' Her sou'wester was dripping wet and her face very pale from the cold and the effort of fighting the relentless waves. This was not a Nain to be trifled with.

Before Gruff could find words to defend himself, a small voice shrieked, 'Gruff's got a sword!' He looked up to see Prem hanging out of his upstairs window, extremely over-excited and not in the least understanding the danger they were all in.

A warning shout came from Tim, over by Rosie's house: 'Big wave coming!'

Deepa and Hardik leapt for the window frame of their cottage and Ffion lunged for the sturdy apple tree at the bottom of their garden. John joined Deepa and Hardik on their window frame and Nain gripped the metal gate of Jack and Dafydd's house, shouting at Gruff to grab something. But instead of finding some way to anchor himself to the land, Gruff turned to face the incoming wave, instinctively raising the sword.

It was a monster. It rolled across the submerged beach, over the sea wall and up to the cottages, hungry and merciless. In its heart Gruff saw Dylan, riding the wave, his arms wide and webbed fingers splayed, his eyes closed and his face a mask of pain and anger and inhuman gut instinct. This was not the Dylan he had spoken to. This was another being entirely. This was a Dylan who didn't even know how deadly he had become.

Gruff's heart quailed and he wanted nothing more than to turn and run, but he stood his ground, sword held high, and braced his body for the impact.

The wave surged to the left at the last moment, an unseen current pushing it away from Gruff and towards Ffion where she was clutching the apple tree. The wave swallowed her whole.

A scream – and there she was, dragged away from the tree like a plucked apple. Gruff raced towards her. The wave reached him at last and he slashed it without thinking as he ran, the sword cleaving a way through the water and freeing up his path.

He threw himself full-length and grabbed the hood of Ffion's jacket, ballooning with water behind her. The sweep of the wave dragged them both out towards the beach and he raised the sword with difficulty and made quick, panicked slices around them, cutting the wave again and again until he felt them slowing just as they reached the sea wall. The wave retreated, empty-handed. Dylan was nowhere to be seen.

Gruff scrambled to his feet and half-dragged Ffion to hers. She found her balance and took his elbow, steering him back the way they had come, her breath coming in small, frightened pants. 'That … sword,' she managed, as they reached the cottages and the flood-fighters came to meet them.

'Yes, it cuts water,' Gruff said.

'Another one!' Rosie screamed, and this time Gruff didn't wait for it to reach him. He turned and raced towards it, leaving behind him aghast cries of, 'Gruff! What are you doing? Come back!'

He met the wave head on, bringing the sword in a great arc around him as far as his arm would stretch. The water punched through beneath and carried him backwards; he stumbled but managed to stay standing. He lurched into a run, slashing his way down the width of the wave, calming the fury of the water before it could reach the cottages. It beat him to Jack and Dafydd's house and took a great chunk from the corner wall, the stones dragged from their moorings and tossed to the ground.

The third wave came on the heels of the last, and Gruff had no time to do anything but raise the sword to shield his head. His feet were swept from beneath him. He heard the guttural roar of tumbling stones mixed with the screams and yells of the flood team as he came down hard on the churned ground and slashed the wave to release himself from its grip.

When he staggered to his feet, he discovered a nightmare. The whole flood team were gone.

Gruff couldn't draw breath. His limbs were heavy with horror. *Nain.*

John, Hardik, Deepa, Ffion, Tim, Jack, Dafydd, Rosie, *Nain.*

'Come back!' Prem's high voice cut through all other sound. 'Come back!'

The little boy pushed through the deep water on his garden path, wide eyes trained on the struggling forms of his parents as they appeared and disappeared in the roiling water. Behind Prem, Elen came splashing with baby Bill strapped to her chest, her arms out to grab him. Iolo burst from the house as well, a bandage round his head and Jack and Dafydd's baby, Rhiannon, in his arms. He was accompanied by the bed-and-breakfast guests, though the man looked like he was close to fainting with pain. 'It's not safe in there!' Iolo yelled. 'There's a great crack – the whole house could come down!'

The sea roared with Dylan's voice: a great, rumbling groan that swelled and rolled and built to a screech. Here came the next wave, full of arms and legs and desperate faces gasping for air.

'Run!' Gruff shouted to Iolo and Elen and the bed-and-breakfast guests. 'Not into a house, get inland!'

They didn't argue. They began to run as best they could: Iolo with Rhiannon; Elen with a screaming, kicking Prem on her hip and a bewildered Bill in the sling; the woman with the hurt man leaning heavily on her shoulders. At first they moved through the knee-deep flood in terrible slow-motion, but then the water was at their shins and then their ankles, and then they were splashing out onto clear grass away from the cottages, staggering against the buffeting wind.

They weren't going to make it to safety. Gruff saw it in the way the sea seemed to buck and vomit the new wave up and out, reaching a long, hungry arm to grab the fleeing figures, the last cottagers standing.

Finish it, or he'll kill us all.

Gruff ran ahead of the wave, its shadow falling across him and bringing with it an overwhelming smell of deep, deep sea. Driftwood and fish and plastic rained on his head as he faced the curve of water arching over him. He leapt as high as he could and slashed left and right before charging into its heaving mass, swiping as he went. Behind him he heard shouts and yelps, but the ferocity of the water was gone, and in one snatched glance Gruff saw that Iolo and the others were safe.

He raced on into the wave, searching for the flood team, desperate to find them before they were dragged back into deeper water. The wave slumped in and down on top of him. He raised the sword and carved a pocket of air, slicing the wave into salty raindrops so that he seemed to be moving through a monsoon-like downpour that pummelled him but left him standing. All was grey-green darkness. He heard the wave closing behind as he walked into its heart, the hilt in his hand fizzing with energy.

A flailing arm broke through into his sanctuary. Gruff reached out with his free hand and clutched a chunk of jacket, pulling hard; Tim slid out of the wave and into the pocket of air, gasping and heaving, water spluttering from his lips. Gruff let him go and concentrated on the sword again as the swell threatened to overwhelm them. 'Move with me!' he yelled over the rush of water and hail of wave-drops. Tim, too shocked to question him, put a hand on Gruff's shoulder and followed him into the wave.

Chapter 33

Ffion was next, swimming straight into Gruff's air bubble and erupting in surprised laughter. She was up on her feet and squeezed in beside Tim before Gruff had to explain what to do, and she reached with her whole upper body through the skin of water and dragged Hardik in to join them.

'Yellow!' Tim shouted in Gruff's ear, and all the hands on his shoulders steered him to the left, Hardik and Ffion now shouting too. 'Yellow! Mair – your nain!'

Gruff saw it. Nain's yellow sou'wester, bright and defiant in the belly of the wave. He ploughed towards the colour as fast as he could, and arms reached past him and grabbed fistfuls of coat, pulling Nain in to safety. Gruff felt a sob of relief rise in him but he swallowed it down. So many still missing. So many still to find.

'To the right!' Nain cried, as soon as she had caught what breath she could. 'I saw Deepa there!'

But even as she spoke, Gruff felt the movement of the wave change. It had been driving towards him and past him as he cut into it but now that force slowed … and paused. For a silent second, all was still.

'Gruff!' Ffion gasped. 'You've got to get behind us!'

The wave smashed into their backs. The four adults stumbled into Gruff and he fell forwards, dropping the sword. It returned instantly to water.

Gruff blundered backwards through the struggling bodies, feeling for the sword hilt. Its cool, writhing surface formed in his palm and he gripped it and slung upwards into the backwash of the wave that was trying to sweep them all out to sea.

The wave was too solid and the sword cuts not deep enough to create a bubble, but he managed to curb the power of it near the ground and find his feet, the four adults clinging onto him and one another. He cut again and again into the water, keeping them all in one place as the wave rushed around them and over them and out to sea. Somewhere in that wave were the people he had not found: Deepa, Jack, Dafydd, Rosie, John. And though Gruff tried not to let the word be thought, it was in every swipe of the sword in front of him: *drowning, drowning, drowning.*

The wave was spent. Gruff stood near the head of the beach, water up to his chest. Tim, Ffion and Hardik helped Nain scramble up the sea wall. Gruff ignored their calls and forced his way down the beach until the water was up to his chin. He held the sword ahead of him, though he could not cut a path through this aimless pool. The sea was gathering itself for another attack. There was no sign of the missing.

Gone. My fault.

Dylan erupted from the water in front of Gruff, his sharp teeth bared. His polluted wound stank, the sickly stench of long-drawn-out agony.

Gruff tried to hold his ground in the heaving water. '*Peidiwch!*' he said. Don't. Salt water slapped into his mouth and he coughed, his words coming out in gasps. 'You've got my friends. You're drowning them. *Please.*'

Dylan showed no sign he had heard. Gruff followed the morgen's storm-filled gaze and saw what had brought him out of the water, understood what was causing the waves to buck and roil in fear and anger.

It was the sword. Gruff was holding it at chest height in front of him, half the blade protruding from the swell. It rippled with glints of light. The last time Dylan had seen this sword, it had been just a hilt and beautiful sounds. Swimming towards it had cost him everything. His sunken eyes were filled now with such hatred, such dread…

Gruff released his grip on the hilt, but even as

he did so, Dylan's webbed hand reached out. In the moment before the sword left Gruff's grasp and melted into water droplets, the morgen's fingers closed around the fluid-soft, steel-sharp blade.

Dylan gasped.

'Sorry! Sorry!' Gruff braced himself and flung his arms up to protect his head, waiting for the sea to thunder down on him in retribution for Dylan's new wound.

The sea did not thunder. In fact, the sea didn't seem to do anything at all.

Gruff raised his head slightly and peered out between his arms.

Dylan was nowhere to be seen. The choppy white horses lessened and lessened until they vanished into tiny ripples. Very slowly – Gruff felt the change, his whole body rocking gently forwards in the subtle shift of power – the sea began to retreat. Out in the open water, the waves were gone.

'What?' Gruff whispered.

The sudden calm brought quiet, and Gruff realised that he could hear calls for help. He turned towards the noise and saw the five lost flood-fighters swimming with exhausted limbs towards the shore.

'YES!' he yelled. The water was only up to his knees now and he started towards the newly-uncovered lifebuoy stand. Hardik and Ffion got there before him and came wading and then swimming with the orange plastic ring to meet the group.

Gruff saw that Rosie and Deepa were supporting John, whose splashing suggested he was not a strong swimmer. Dafydd had his husband Jack in a lifeguard's hold, his hand under his chin, and Gruff's heart tightened horribly – but when Hardik and Ffion arrived with the ring, Jack grabbed it himself and Gruff heard him half-laugh and say, 'Leg cramp. I'm okay.'

Rosie and Deepa brought John to the ring, then they and Dafydd joined Hardik and Ffion swimming to shore. Tim, Nain and the bed-and-breakfast guests pulled the life ring's rope, hand over hand, dragging their catch to safety.

Gruff headed towards them all, relief making his legs wobbly. There was no water round him now. The tideline was almost back to where it ought to be, leaving seaweed and crabs and rubbish strewn on the sand.

And something else. Something like a man, but not a man. Something beached, something helpless. A sprawling figure with webbed feet and hands and dull grey scales, abandoned by the water.

Gruff stopped. 'Dylan?' he called.

No movement.

'Dylan?' Gruff ran down the beach towards the motionless figure. He thumped to his knees at the morgen's side. 'Are you okay?' he asked.

Dylan opened his eyes and looked straight at Gruff. He managed a tiny smile of recognition, and Gruff could see that this Dylan was the one he had talked to at the Sleepers, not the one who had caused the storm. This Dylan knew who Gruff was, and would listen to him when he spoke.

Dylan was making a small, rhythmic choking noise in the back of his throat. Gruff winced. 'You can't breathe.' He scooped his hands under Dylan's ragged body and lifted him without thinking. Internal waves lapped up Gruff's arms. The morgen was lighter than he had expected, no heavier than Prem.

As he stumbled to his feet, Dylan in his arms, Gruff heard a steady dribbling sound that made his heart lurch. 'You're bleeding,' he said, and he looked for the deep cuts he was sure Dylan had suffered from clutching the sword blade. But there were no wounds.

There were no wounds, because there was no hand.

Gruff concentrated hard on not letting his knees collapse beneath him.

Dylan's arm stopped at the elbow. Instead of a

bloody stump, clear water bubbled from it, as though he was an ice sculpture melting in the sun.

Dylan began to shudder and retch. Gruff came to his senses and half-ran down the beach into shallow water. He pushed on until the gentle waves were at his shaking knees, and then knelt and placed Dylan down, submerging him fully.

As Gruff withdrew his arms, Dylan's remaining hand found his and took it in a cold, scaly-soft grasp. Gruff sat cross-legged, the water up to his chin, and waited for Dylan to find the breath and energy to speak. He needed to know what had happened. He needed to know if he could help. Gentle wavelets washed from Dylan to Gruff, mirroring the calm sea around them.

The wind had died to a whisper. Overhead, the clouds were thinning and burning up in the heat of the morning sun. The storm was the memory of a nightmare.

Gruff thought of the lifeboat, and tried not to think of the lifeboat. He thought of Mat, and wished she would pop up next to him, grinning and safe.

Dylan's grip grew tighter as his strength returned. At last his face appeared above the surface and he looked at Gruff with smiling eyes imbued with a gentle swell.

'I didn't know the sword had this power,' Dylan said.

'Me neither.'

'And Gofannon can't have known,' Dylan added, 'or she would have instructed you to do deliberately what was done by accident.'

'But what *have* I done?' Gruff's stomach clenched and unclenched, bile rising in his throat. Was Dylan disintegrating because of him?

Dylan smiled. 'You held the sword, and I touched the blade. It's forged with magic and I'm not mortal. Instead of cutting me, it's severed me from this decaying body.'

'But does that mean…' Gruff licked his salt-cracked lips. 'I – I've killed you? I didn't mean to! I tried to drop the sword, I…'

Dylan squeezed Gruff's hand. 'You haven't killed me. You have given me my life.'

Gruff saw that Dylan's arm was now entirely gone. His chest, and the terrible ancient wound there, bubbled gradually away in a spring of clear water that spread down his legs and crept up towards his neck.

'You have saved me,' Dylan said, and his voice seemed to strengthen even as he melted away. 'You've ended a storm that began long ago. And you fought me bravely today, wielding that sword – you and the morgen I haven't met; she was out here too, wasn't she? I sensed the calm she spread through my anger. You saved lives when I would have taken them. You stopped me accomplishing what I never intended to do.'

Gruff thought of the lifeboat carrying Dad and Zosia and all the others, of the boat they had gone to rescue, of Mat swimming out into the tempest alone. *I hope so*, he thought.

'I am one with the sea,' Dylan whispered. He closed his eyes as his body merged with the rippling water. 'I am home.'

Dylan's webbed, scaly grip rushed out from between Gruff's fingers and then there was just his face, upturned to the sky, his lips quirked into a smile of playfulness and peace.

Then Dylan was gone, and Gruff sat alone in the shallows.

Chapter 34

Gruff sat there for some time, listening to the calls and laughter behind him as the survivors of the final Wounded Sea storm set about the long job of cleaning up. He collected the pieces of rubbish that had melted from Dylan's wound – a scrap of fishing net and a plastic bag, a bottle cap, a disposable latex glove – and held them, washed clean by the sea. Then he waded ashore and placed them up on the coast path with the rest of the storm rubbish that was being collected, ready to be sorted and recycled.

Nain descended on him, dressed in a dry pair of trousers and a checked shirt that were obviously borrowed from Iolo. 'You … I'm so angry … I'm … thank you.' She pulled him into a tight, tight hug. 'You brave boy. And I saw you just now, out there, with him – was that him? Is he gone?'

Gruff nodded. 'He's gone. He's free.'

One after another, and sometimes two or three at a time, the other adults came over to give him soggy, laughing hugs, heady with relief and joy for their lives.

Only John was quiet, and he drew Gruff and Nain to one side.

'What about Matty?' he whispered. 'What about my Mat and the lifeboat?'

Gruff could only shake his head. 'I don't know.'

'Mat?' Nain snapped, shocked. 'You don't mean she's –'

'News!' Iolo hurried up to them, waving his walkie-talkie. 'The lifeboat's safe, and all on board her. They're escorting the fishing boat they went to help back to Trefynys – it was Gareth Jones and his son out there, but all safe now.'

Relief burst in Gruff's chest. 'What about Mat?' he and John asked as one.

Iolo's grin turned slowly to confusion. 'Mat? Surely she didn't go out with the boat?'

John and Gruff exchanged glances. 'No,' John said eventually. 'She didn't.'

Gruff searched for words, to help himself as well as John. 'She should be fine,' he said. 'So long as she keeps on being Mat the morgen. She'll be okay. She can breathe underwater.'

Nain gasped and Iolo's eyes fairly popped out of his head. 'What?' he yelped. 'Mat can *what* now?'

Gruff left John to explain and ran back to the water. 'Dylan!' he shouted. 'I don't know if you can hear me, but my friend Mat, the morgen, is still out there somewhere. Is she okay? Do you know if she's okay?'

The waves sucked and shushed innocently, the morning sun glinting off their edges.

'Dylan!' Gruff called again. *Dylan Ail Don, ni thorrodd don o dano erioed; a wnewch chi siarad â mi?*'

Gruff counted his heartbeats. Five. Ten. Fifteen. Hope ebbed quietly away with the retreating tide.

But then the water a few feet from him began to swirl and pulse with invisible life. Gruff ran forwards, splashing through the shallows. The disturbance was around him, little eddies and whirlpools swishing in the stillness. It looked a little like a meeting of deep water currents, where fish are brought to the surface and seals and gulls feast, but it was only as wide as Gruff's outstretched arms. The droplets of Dylan, brought together at Gruff's call.

'Hello,' Gruff said, hoping that this new form of Dylan could understand him. 'I'm worried about Mat. She's the morgen who went to help the lifeboat but she hasn't come back. I just want to know she's okay.'

The eddying water quickened, taking on a new urgency. It tugged at Gruff, seeming to want to carry him away.

Do I trust him? Gruff thought. And then, *Yes.* He pushed off from the sand into a front crawl. Dylan's droplets gathered themselves around him and sped him out from the beach.

They swam together away from the cottages, past the headland and round the coast. Swimming with Dylan was like flying. Gruff brought his arms round and kicked his legs like he normally would, but the power around him surged him forwards as though he was turbocharged. He grinned with exhilaration and wondered if this was how Mat felt when she swam as a morgen.

Gruff sensed a change in their direction and looked up to see that they were entering the bay that held the jetty and the lifeboat station. There was no movement at the station – the lifeboat was still escorting Gareth Jones's fishing boat back to Trefynys.

'Is she here?' Gruff whispered to the water. Even as he asked the question, he felt the purpose of the droplets around him fading and saw a dark head that was not a seal bobbing in the middle of the bay. It was her. Mat was here; Mat was safe.

'*Diolch! Diolch*, Dylan. Thank you, thank you, thank you!'

The morgen had brought him to the morgen. The swirling, energised water dispersed and Dylan returned to the sea.

Chapter 35

Gruff swam to the jetty, clumsy and splashing in his excitement. 'Mat!' he called. 'Mat! You're okay!' He grabbed the end of the jetty and hauled himself out onto the wooden planks. He was shaking; his pent-up worry released into pure joy. Everyone was safe. The storm was over, and everyone was safe.

He crawled along the wet boards until he was on a level with Mat, bobbing in the bay. He waved wildly. 'Mat! You're safe! Come out and show John you're safe – he's so worried.'

Mat turned to face him and Gruff's heart clenched tight. Her eyes were filled with roiling waves, as wild and unpredictable as the storm they had survived.

Gruff held out his hand as though coaxing a nervous cat. 'Do you remember me?'

Mat stared. After a long moment of stillness, she coasted slowly towards him and stopped a few metres away, still staring as though he was the strangest creature she had ever encountered.

'I'm Gruff,' he said clearly, though he could feel his pulse in his throat and thought he might choke on it. 'I'm Gruffydd ap Owain, remember? And you're Matylda Kowalska.'

Mat blinked water-washed eyes. There was no recognition in her gaze, only curiosity.

'You remembered!' Gruff snapped, frustrated. 'You helped me save the sheep. You talked to me. You went out to save the lifeboat.'

'There was a boat,' Mat said solemnly. 'It was in trouble. The people were in trouble. But I calmed the sea and the people are safe now.'

'Yes!' Gruff clung to her words as John and Jack had clung to the life ring. 'Do you remember who was on the boat, Mat?'

'People.'

'Your *mum*, Mat. Your *mum*. My *dad*. Don't you remember?'

'Are you calling me Mat?'

Gruff buried his head in his hands. 'Yes!' he shouted. 'Please remember! Look – never mind. Forget remembering. Just take my hand, okay? Come ashore.'

He stretched his hand out towards her. Mat flinched and for a terrible moment Gruff thought he had scared her off – that she would swim away and that would be it. He held his breath and kept very still.

Slowly, uncertainly, Mat swam closer and brought her hand up to his. Waves rushed up Gruff's arm and pulsed around his ribcage. He grasped Mat's fingers tightly, relieved to find there was no webbing there yet, no scales on her skin.

'Are you going to come out of the water?' he asked.

Mat the morgen nodded, her curiosity getting the better of her. Gruff put his other hand out and helped her clamber onto the jetty next to him.

Almost immediately, Mat began to choke. Her eyes bulged and she scrabbled at her gills, at her face, at Gruff's hands and arms – she tried to pull away, back into the water, but Gruff held her tightly. 'Stay here! Just breathe through your mouth and nose. Remember how to do it – you've done it your whole life! Come on!'

Mat thrashed in his grasp. Her eyes were unfocused now, every scrap of energy in her body grappling for breath. Doubt sledgehammered into Gruff's resolve. He was suffocating her.

He heaved her over the side of the jetty and she hit the water like a dead weight. Gruff's own breath came ragged and scared now. Mat sank out of sight.

She rose up again, anger in every feature. 'You tried to kill me.'

'No!' Gruff shook his head so hard he hurt himself. 'I'm trying to help you. You're not a morgen, Mat. You're a human. You've got to come home.'

Something like pain flashed across her face. 'Home.'

'Home,' he repeated, crossing his fingers tightly. Was her memory stirring?

'I don't belong,' Mat said slowly.

'What?'

'This is *your* home, Gruff.'

'YES!' Gruff punched the air. 'You remember me!' But then her words caught up with him. 'Wait – what?'

'The island,' Mat said, 'is your home. It isn't mine, is it? I don't belong anywhere.'

'Yes, you do,' Gruff began, thoroughly confused now.

'Where do I fit?' Mat's voice was as lost as an echo that had forgotten who made it.

'Here,' Gruff said firmly. 'With Zosia and John. With the people you love. That's where home is. You told me that. And Dad told me too. You said the island's my home, but I might not even live here much longer.' He hesitated, thinking of the sheep he had saved – would they be someone else's flock soon? He swallowed. 'My home is with Dad and Nain. Yours is with Zosia and John.'

Mat's story on the island was only just beginning, but Gruff's may have already run its course. He'd been so jealous of Mat when she first arrived. Had she been able to tell? Had his jealousy made her feel unwelcome? Was she choosing water because he had not wanted her on land?

Gruff gathered up the last of that jealousy and threw it from him in disgust. The island was Mat's home, as much as it had ever been his.

'Think of your mum and John,' he said. 'Come home. Please.'

Mat's face twisted in distress. 'I love them!' she shouted. 'I do! I don't want to leave them. But if I stay near the island, they'll still be here so we'll still be together, and –'

'You're not seriously going to choose the water? Don't be ridiculous.'

Mat bared her teeth and Gruff remembered that he wasn't talking to the Mat he knew. This was Mat the morgen, and she saw the world in a different way to the Mat who had arrived on the island just a few days earlier. The Mat who breathed air and was his friend.

'Please remember who you were,' Gruff said softly.

She was silent for a long time. When she finally

spoke her voice shook with held-back tears. 'I feel at home in the water. More at home than I've ever felt. Where do I belong, anyway? I started off in Poland but I don't even remember that; I've lived in seven places in eleven years, been to four different schools. And the only thing that's been the same is the pull of the sea always and always. So where do I belong?'

'Here.' Gruff reached his hand out once more. 'You belong here, on this island.' The truth of his words built in him. 'Home is where you choose it to be, Mat. It's your choice.'

He remembered Dylan's question before the storm. *Will she choose the water?*

Gruff met the untethered sea in Mat's gaze. 'Please, Mat. Choose the land.'

He lay down on his front on the jetty, reached below the surface and found Mat's cold hand. Her waves washed up his arm and surrounded his heart, pulsing against it with every beat. Was this what Mat had felt like her whole life, the sea pounding and pounding inside her, never letting her truly belong?

Silent tears streamed down Mat's face.

Gruff squeezed her limp fingers. 'Home is where you choose to make it, Mat.'

The waves beating against his heart sucked and spat ... and lessened. The water link with Mat was now a soft swell, now a retreating tide, now a trickle, now...

Nothing.

Mat choked and gasped. She gripped Gruff's hand tightly. 'Jetty,' she croaked. 'Jetty.'

Gruff hesitated. Shouldn't Mat submerge if she was unable to breathe?

But Mat was surging forwards out of the water herself. She scrambled up onto the wooden boards and curled into a ball on her side, hacking and coughing. Gruff crouched beside her, panic taking hold. 'Mat, you can't breathe!'

Mat's voice came in gasps: 'I ... choose ... land.'

And she was still.

The sudden silence sliced through Gruff like a knife. 'No!' he whispered. 'No, no, no...'

Mat's eyes were closed. The silence was a hundred times worse than her desperate choking. Gruff dragged her towards the edge of the jetty, intending to get her down into the water, but even as he did so he saw that her gills had sealed themselves. The flaps of skin were closed by thin white scars, as though they were old wounds, long ago healed. The way back to the sea was barred.

Mind blank with fear, Gruff laid Mat on her back and desperately tried to remember what he had seen on TV shows when people had to give CPR. How long had she not been breathing? He didn't dare think. He put his hands on top of one another in the centre of Mat's chest and pumped down, hard.

Mat's eyes flew open. 'Ow!' She sat up and rubbed her ribs. 'What did you do that for?'

Chapter 36

Nain and John, bearing towels, found them just as the lifeboat turned into the bay. Dad and Zosia joined the group once the boat was set to rights, and Gruff began to feel as flat as a pancake from all the hugging.

'It was the strangest thing,' Zosia said, 'but there was a seal out there, believe it or not. What it was doing, swimming so close to the boats in that storm, I don't know. I think it was our lucky seal. Every time I saw it, it was as though the waves got calmer.'

Gruff caught Mat's eye.

'*Matylda*,' Zosia gasped, properly registering the state of her towel-wrapped daughter for the first time. 'You're *soaked*! You weren't outside in that storm? And ... are you wearing a *wetsuit*?'

'Um,' Mat said.

'Now's the time, Matty,' John smiled. 'I think we might need to know all.'

Gruff left Mat to it and pulled Dad and Nain on ahead as they began the walk back to the farmhouse. 'What was that all about?' Dad asked. He looked sideways at Gruff. 'And I'm really hoping you're not wearing your wetsuit because you went in the sea.'

'Er…'

'All right, Gruffydd ap Owain,' Nain said sternly. 'Out with it.'

So Gruff came out with it.

*

Everyone mucked in for the Great Clean-Up. Furniture was dragged out of the fishermen's cottages and cleaned and treated to rescue it from the salt water; walls were repaired, roofs re-tiled, chimneys rebuilt. Two builders travelled over from the mainland for the trickier bits, paid for by the disaster fund that everyone on the island contributed to in case of times like this. Protected by cliffs, the town side of the island had fared much better. Although all the boats in the harbour needed bailing out and the pub's sign was blown down, the inhabitants (apart from those on the lifeboat crew) had not realised just how ferocious the storm had been.

The weaker lambs had to be helped to eat until they were strong enough to stand. Three of the adult sheep – Frank, Greta and Hetty – came down with pneumonia. Dad went to the vets on the mainland

and bought antibiotics, which had to be administered every day. Gruff also administered crusts of bread. Frank, Greta and Hetty decided they liked him a lot.

Two bags of fleece in the wool barn had been drenched when a window blew in. Gruff discovered this soon after the storm and unpacked the bags, letting the fleeces dry out before they rotted like the bags of Gotland fleeces had the winter before. Roof tiles were down, three of the solar panels were beyond repair and the barn door needed fixing. The dry stone wall that the seventh Sleeper had ploughed through had to be rebuilt. The farm's share of the disaster fund helped them with some of the things, but did not stretch to all of it. And every day spent helping out at the fishermen's cottages was a day that the wool barn stood empty and the fleece preparation stood still – but then, Gruff found himself thinking, without customers the fleece might as well remain untouched.

He knew that the farm was hanging on by a thread, and he could see Dad and Nain knew it too. They did not talk about it. They helped with the Great Clean-Up and enjoyed what time they had left.

On the fifth morning after the storm, Mat found Gruff waterproofing Iolo's windowsill and thrust a piece of paper into his hand.

Gruff stared blankly at it. It looked like a draft copy of a poster or a leaflet. There were no pictures, but blank squares had things like 'History of the farm' and 'Order form' written inside them. 'What is it?' Gruff asked, putting his paintbrush down.

'It's a website.' Mat was fizzing with excitement. 'Mama and John do online marketing, right?'

'Er … okay.' Gruff didn't really know what Zosia and John did. He just knew that computer programming was involved.

'This storm,' Mat said, 'is the best thing that could have happened to you.'

Gruff snorted.

'No, really.' Mat pointed to a box that said 'Storm Dylan'. 'It's perfect! You have an *angle*.'

Gruff made a face. 'An angle?'

'Mama and John are always looking for the 'angle' in stuff, and I knew you were really worried about the farm, and I just thought…' She began to trail off, sounding more unsure. 'I mean, it seemed like a good idea. I thought of it yesterday, when I was helping Rosie rebuild her chimney … and it's just, well … if you get your story out there, people will notice you and might want to buy from you. The storm's a good story. And so's the fact you farm on an island, and you try really hard to be carbon neutral. I talked to

Mama and John, and they're happy to help you create a website, and social media accounts.'

Gruff shook his head, feeling suddenly hot and embarrassed. He gave Mat the website draft and picked up his paintbrush, turning back to the windowsill. 'We can't pay for that. Sorry.'

'But you don't need to pay for it.'

Gruff paused with his paintbrush dipped in the waterproofing paint. 'What?'

'Mama and John know everything,' Mat said. 'Not just about me being a morgen; they know what happened at the jetty, too.' She fiddled with one of her plaits and her voice grew quieter. 'I nearly swam away and forgot about everyone I love. But you stopped me.'

Gruff didn't like to think about what had happened at the jetty. The memory of those terrible moments after Mat had stopped breathing through her gills and before she had begun to breathe through her mouth and nose leapt out at him whenever he had a moment alone.

Mat saw the look on his face. 'Stop worrying,' she said. They had already had many conversations about what had happened that day – and what might have happened. '*I* was the one who made the choice that meant my gills closed up. But you reminded me I had a choice. You saved me.' She shrugged and smiled. 'I told Mama and John about that, and now they think you can do no wrong. Anyway, they liked you and your family before any of this happened. They don't want you to lose the farm.' She grinned and waved the website draft under his nose. 'So. What do you think?'

Gruff felt a smile tugging at his mouth, and he gave in to a flicker of hope. 'I think we're really lucky you came to live here.'

Mat laughed. 'I think so too!'

Chapter 37

'Smile, Guinevere,' Gruff said. He was sitting cross-legged on a sheep-poo-free patch of grass, the camera he and Mat had borrowed from Tim ('If you scratch it or drop it in the sea, I will actually have your guts for garters, and enjoy wearing them to hold my socks up') levelled carefully at the grazing sheep. At the sound of his voice, Guinevere raised her head and looked at him. *What?* the look said. *Have you got bread for me? If not then move along, please.*

'Very photogenic,' Mat said, glancing at the digital display over Gruff's shoulder. 'You're right, it's much better quality than your phone.' She had a notebook in her lap and was sketching. 'How's this? The "Meet the Sheep" feature can have pictures and facts for each sheep, like Top Trump cards. And we can have the front page set up so it changes every day to be a different cover sheep.'

'Guinevere won't like sharing the glory,' Gruff grinned. 'Her social media following is already going to her head.' He trained the camera on Daisy, who had a daisy sticking out of her mouth.

'Perfect!' Mat laughed.

Gruff turned the camera off and returned it carefully to its soft black carry case. He put the case down on the grass next to the blacksmith's hammer and watched Mat scribble in her notebook. He'd taken to bringing the hammer everywhere he and Mat went. He had a feeling that the blacksmith would be back one day to reclaim it, and that they should keep it safe until then.

'What should Guinevere have under "fun fact"?' Mat asked.

'Best escaper,' Gruff said immediately. 'She knows she gets bread to lure her back, so she's always doing it. And there were loads of shares on that compilation video of her jumping over walls.'

'Master of escape,' Mat said, writing it down. 'Plans ahead. Gets what she wants.'

He laughed. 'Yep, that's Guinevere!'

Mat chewed the end of her pencil, looking over her design with a critical eye.

'Have you heard back from that environmental diving charity?' Gruff asked.

'Yeah, they've got them on their list.' Mat had seen four abandoned fishing nets underwater in her morgen state but not been able to release them from the lobster pots, rocks and wrecked fishing boat they had been tangled in. They were a hazard for sea creatures that could get caught in them.

'So what do they do with them?'

'They can be recycled into plastic pellets that are used to make other stuff, like shoes.'

'That's amazing!'

'Yeah, it is.'

They sat in silence for a while, watching a group of lambs play racing games up and down the line of the stone wall. Gruff felt every bit as happy as those lambs. The main body of the website was up and running, including an exciting description of the storm and the sheep's rescue, and pictures and videos on social media had done really well. There had already been two new outlets who had got in touch with them to order stock. Nain and Dad's anxious, muttered conversations about the accounts were fewer, and the worried frowns they had carried for so many weeks were replaced by smiles. They had hope again.

Gruff heard soft footsteps approaching, and the flap of material. *That's a cloak*, he thought, remembering the sound. A shiver went down his spine. 'She's here,' he whispered.

Mat glanced at him. 'What?'

The blacksmith's voice was directly behind them.

'*Dw i ddim yn gwybod eich enwau.*' I don't know your names.

Gruff and Mat scrambled to their feet and spun round. The blacksmith stood there, tall and solid and real in the grey light of the cloudy afternoon. Soot on her face and her clothes, fresh mud on her boots, windswept hair. She looked at them both with a smile so warm she seemed to glow.

'*Gruff dw i,*' Gruff said. He nudged Mat and said, 'She wants our names.'

'I'm Mat,' Mat whispered, and Gruff remembered this was the first time she had seen the blacksmith.

'I am Gofannon,' the blacksmith said in English.

Gruff had never seen Gofannon look so happy. Without her worry she was someone new. 'You're not on the seventh Sleeper,' he said.

Gofannon shook her head. 'I'm free,' she replied. '*We're* free, Dylan and I both. And we have the two of you to thank for that.'

'We can't pull the sword from the sea anymore,' Mat said. 'We've both tried.'

'No.' Gofannon bent down and picked up the hammer from the grass, weighing it in her hand. 'It was never really meant for this world. But you will be able to wield it again, if you ever need to.'

Mat grinned. 'Like Excalibur.'

Gofannon laughed. 'Perhaps.' She slotted the hammer into her tool belt.

'Will we see you again?' Gruff asked. 'Is Dylan happy?'

'I don't know if we'll meet again,' Gofannon said. 'We do not live to the same time as one another. But be assured that Dylan is happier than you can imagine.'

'I'm glad,' Gruff said quietly.

He hesitated, then asked the question that had been bothering the edge of his mind since he had first seen Gofannon standing on the seventh Sleeper. 'Why was it me who saw you? And why could I feel the sea in Mat, when other people couldn't?'

'I can't be sure,' Gofannon said. 'Sometimes people have seen me, and sometimes they haven't. But I believe that empathy has a part to play. You're aware of the feelings of others, so you sensed Mat's restlessness, and my desperation to be seen and heard.'

'Yes!' Mat said. 'That makes sense. You're thoughtful, Gruff. You're kind.'

Gruff shrugged, embarrassed. 'So are you.'

A memory had been stirring at the back of his thoughts and as he looked for an escape route from talking about himself, it shot suddenly into focus. 'Gofannon!' he said. 'I remember Taid telling me a story about you. Was it you? Something in *Culhwch ac Olwen*, the story with King Arthur in it. There was a whole list of stuff the knights had to do, like a quest...'

Gruff stopped, sadness stepping out to greet him. It had been one of Taid's favourite stories to tell. He had always brought the far-off world to vivid life: the ancient, talking salmon; the giant Ysbaddaden; the ferocious boar named Twrch Trwyth...

Gofannon nodded. 'I play a small part in that tale. Your grandfather remembers well.'

Gruff smiled, his sadness mixed with pride. 'He did. His stories were the best. And Nain's are, too.'

'And yours will be,' Gofannon said. 'The stories you learn and the stories you live through.' Her smile widened. 'And now, thanks to you both, I can at last cross the bridge and go home to Annwn to tell my own story there. Thank you, Gruff. Thank you, Mat, the morgen who chose land.'

Mat grinned. 'Definitely the right choice.' She shrugged. 'I'm sad to lose the wave calming thing though. That was pretty great, and it'd be useful as an oceanologist!'

Mischief twinkled across Gofannon's face. 'What makes you so sure you've lost it?'

Mat's mouth dropped open. 'Can I? Without turning into a morgen again?'

'You've made your choice and you're of the land now. But you will always be a morgen, too.'

Mat bounced up and down with excitement. 'Awesome!'

Gofannon laughed and turned to Gruff. 'Goodbye, Gruff. You heard me when no one else could.'

'*Hwyl fawr*,' Gruff said. Goodbye.

'*Hwyl fawr*,' Gofannon smiled. She turned and walked away from them with long-legged strides: across Top Field, over the hurdle blocking the Weeping Stone's hole in the wall, across the coast path and down onto the beach.

She waded out to the first of the Sleepers, climbed up it, and jumped from stone to stone until she stood on the seventh. She turned back towards the land and raised one arm in farewell. Gruff and Mat waved.

Gofannon dropped her arm, turned to face the open sea, and stepped off the seventh Sleeper. She vanished before she hit the water.

Mat breathed in sharply. 'Where did she go?' she whispered.

Gruff grinned. 'Home.' Joy bubbled up inside him and he grabbed Mat's hands and spun round with her, faster and faster.

Mat laughed. 'Home!' she shouted to the grey clouds and a passing tern.

They fell over and lay on their backs on the grass, breathless and giggling. Gruff closed his eyes and listened to the crunching munching of the grazing sheep, the busy buzzing of a bee, the rhythmic swoosh of the waves. He took a deep breath that smelled of sheep and salt and gorse blossom.

Thundering hooves reverberated through the ground. A white shape barrelled past them and leapt clean over the dry stone wall onto the coast path.

'Sheep out!' Dad shouted from somewhere over by the farmhouse.

Gruff and Mat grinned at one another. 'On it!' Gruff yelled back, and together they set off in pursuit of Guinevere, Master of Escape.

Acknowledgements

Thank you to everyone at Firefly, especially to Janet Thomas and Rebecca F. John, my hawk-eyed and thoughtful editors, Amy Low for their brilliant and supportive marketing work and illustrator Laura Borio and designer Becka Moor for this wonderful cover. Thank you to my lovely agent Abi Sparrow for championing my stories.

This book first began to take shape on the MA in Writing for Young People course at Bath Spa University in 2015-16, and I'd like to thank everyone on that course, tutors and students alike, for their support, insight and enthusiasm. I am so lucky to have found such a wonderful writing community. Thanks especially to Elen Caldecott, who supervised the first version of this story during the MA, when it was a very different tale but with similar bones! When I began the story all over again, the encouragement and perceptive critiques of Catherine, Julia and Kat during our video-call writing workshops helped so much.

Thank you, Jane, for helping me with my Welsh, and for coming up with some truly beautiful language choices. Thank you, Ola, for your invaluable assistance with the Polish elements in the story. And thank you to my ever-supportive family and friends, and to all the readers who have read drafts of my stories over the years and encouraged me to keep at it.

This is a story inspired by myth

Dylan and Gofannon are both characters from old Welsh mythology, and as well as popping up in medieval poetry they both appear in the collection of tales known as the Mabinogion – Dylan in the fourth branch of the Mabinogi and Gofannon in *Culhwch ac Olwen*. In fact, the words Gruff uses to call Dylan are based on the original medieval Welsh description of Dylan in the fourth branch, which I read in the edition by Ian Hughes. If you'd like to discover more of these old tales, I can highly recommend *The Mab: Eleven Epic Stories from the Mabinogi*, edited by Matt Brown and Eloise Williams, and my favourite translation of the original medieval stories is that of Sioned Davies. Every myth holds fresh story sparks.

Beatrice Wallbank grew up in mid-Wales, surrounded by sheep. When not wandering about in wild places thinking about stories, she works backstage in theatre, storytelling in a different form. She also really likes Old Stuff and is a historian of things relating to the sea in early medieval Wales.

The Sleeping Stones is her first book. Beatrice is based near Newtown.

At Firefly we care very much about the environment and our responsibility to it. Many of our stories, such as this one, involve the natural world, our place in it and what we can all do to help it, and us, survive the challenges of the climate emergency. Go to our website www.fireflypress.co.uk to find more of our great stories that focus on the environment, like *The Territory*, *Aubrey and the Terrible Ladybirds*, *The Song that Sings Us* and *My Name is River*.

As a Wales-based publisher we are also very proud of the beautiful natural places, plants and animals in our country on the western side of Great Britain.

We are always looking at reducing our impact on the environment, including our carbon footprint and the materials we use, and are taking part in UK-wide publishing initiatives to improve this wherever we can.